CALL TO HER HEART

The butler tapped on Amory's door and told her some-one wished to speak to her on the telephone.

"Hello! Is that you, Miss Lorrimer? Amory?" came a strong voice with a lilt in it.

Now who could that be? And then she knew and a thrill came to her heart. It was Gareth!

"Well, I'm hopping off, and I just wanted you to know that if anything happens it's all right with me the way you said."

"Oh!" she said with a choking sound to her voice as if the tears were coming, "Oh, I'm glad!"

"Good-by—" his voice trailed off chokily, "Dar—!"

Was that "Darling" he had said? "Good-by, Darling!"

A wave of gladness surged over her, made up of fear and joy and hope, and still that soft word chimed over in her heart, "Darling! Darling! Darling!"

Bantam Books by Grace Livingston Hill
Ask your bookseller for the books you have missed

GRACE
LIVINGSTON
HILL

SILVER WINGS

BANTAM BOOKS
TORONTO · NEW YORK · LONDON

SILVER WINGS

*A Bantam Book / published by arrangement with
J. B. Lippincott Company*

PRINTING HISTORY
*Lippincott-edition published 1931
Bantam edition / November 1973*
2nd printing .... May 1974   3rd printing .. November 1974
4th printing ...... January 1980

ISBN 0-553-13674-7

Published simultaneously in the United States and Canada

---

*Bantam Books are published by Bantam Books, Inc. Its trade-
mark, consisting of the words "Bantam Books" and the por-
trayal of a bantam, is Registered in U.S. Patent and Trademark
Office and in other countries. Marca Registrada. Bantam
Books, Inc., 666 Fifth Avenue, New York, New York 10019.*

COVER PRINTED IN THE UNITED STATES OF AMERICA
TEXT PRINTED IN CANADA

CHAPTER I

AMORY had walked from the station to save the taxi fare, but had she realized the distance even her courageous heart might have hesitated.

"Third mansion on the right, not the third residence—" the cryptic station agent had advised her tersely, and Amory visioned a possible row of neat two story bricks, with larger houses beyond set in wide lawns. She picked up her suit case briskly and stepped off down the elm shaded road. Her trunk would follow later.

The street opened out amply and leisurely with no houses at all for some distance, nothing but green fields edged by neat hedges. Then a large old fashioned brick house emerged in glimpses through the trees. It was set far back in a well kept lawn, with a flower garden at one side. She paused and studied it. Was this a residence or a mansion? Had she possibly made a mistake and turned the wrong way at the station? But no, the agent had been watching her. He would surely have told her if she had been wrong. She gave the brick house another appraising glance and revised her ideas of residences and incidentally of Briarcliffe. If such palaces as this one on her right were mere residences what would the mansions be? And if she had come to take up her abode in a mansion would the modest wardrobe contained in her small shabby suit case, and her small shabby trunk suffice, even for a social secretary? Somewhat apprehensively she went on, and presently passed a big white colonial house enmeshed by a labyrinth of small box hedges. Two lovely stone houses were next, built long and low like bungalows, with arched lattices covered with roses in bloom. And cozy home-like gardens. Well, at least these were not mansions, and still, they spoke of wealth. Perhaps the agent meant these were not to be counted and the first two must have been mansions. That was it probably.

The next place was Norman in architecture, and she decided it was the third mansion and walked confidently up the drive and rang the door bell. But the maid who answered the door answered curtly that the Whitneys did not live there. She did not know where they lived. She was new at the place, and the folks were all out.

Amory went back to the street again and stood bewildered but finally decided to go on, as there was no one in sight whom she could ask.

The next house was another colonial, smaller than the first, and she hardly knew whether to class it as a mansion or not. Three more houses she passed doubtfully, and then another large stone house ostentatious with awnings and a wide orange and black umbrella spread over a tea table on the lawn.

There were some children playing about a fountain, and a man was cutting the hedge about the terrace. She decided to try again.

The children only stared when she asked them but the man turned from his work and told her:

"It's some ways up the pike, lady. The third large mansion on yer right—" he said.

"But which is the first mansion?" she asked in despair setting down the suit case which now was making her feel its every pound. "Do you count from here, or where?"

The man looked at her as if she were an ignoramus, but answered good-naturedly:

"There's two more 'ouses, lady, beyont this, an' then ye come to the big *hes*tates. It's the third one of them, ma'am, the third *hes*tate!"

Amory thanked him and picked up her suit case, but as she went wearily down the walk she was possessed by a desire to laugh aloud. So she was going to an "*hes*tate"! What would Aunt Hannah say to that? What would Rayport think if they knew? How Helen and Miriam and Esther would exclaim wistfully! How far removed she felt herself already! Could she stand it, this new world that seemed at just this glimpse like another universe? What part had she in a world like this? Oh, of course she had come to work, and not to have part in the life at all; but already the little lonesome part of her that lived and loved, felt suddenly appalled at the wide difference there would be between this new life and the precious one she had left behind in the quaint loving friendly home town where she had been brought up by her two dear maiden aunts.

But this would not do. She must not get maudlin before she arrived. She was here to earn good hard money to help get Aunt Hannah the nurse and the specialist she needed, and to provide a lot of necessities to make it easier for frail little Aunt Jocelyn now that she was not to be there to save her from the hard knocks of life. So she was to live in a mansion! Well, she might have known it from the size of the salary the Whitneys were willing to pay. It was nothing short of a miracle that such a salary had fallen to her lot! If it hadn't been for the minister who used to know Mr. Whitney in college days, and happened to meet him on a trip to town and find out he was looking for a social secretary for his wife, she never would have got it of course. And now the difficulty would be to keep it! And then for the thousandth time she was visited by her fears. Yet of course, she *was* good at dictation. Hadn't she taken the prize in the contest? And of course the Rayport Seminary had had a marvelous advantage over other small town schools, in having had as principal for five years a woman of national reputation. She had come to Rayport as a special dispensation for a period to be near her old mother who was slowly dying of an incurable trouble and could not be moved without great suffering. Well all those things would count—she must just do her best.

At last she passed the next two big houses, and a great stone wall with immense corner pillars, vine clad and rose capped, announced the beginning of the first "*hes*tate." Far ahead of her, as if they were miles away, loomed more pillars. When she came to them in her weary plodding they proved to be furnished with iron grill work that gave a glimpse of a far white marble building which fully bore out the name mansion.

Amory put her suit case down and sat on it for a few minutes to rest in the shadow of this great gateway. She felt like a very little pilgrim indeed as she looked wistfully through the iron gates and studied the beautiful palace in the distance, wondering if the Whitney place would be anything like it.

Suddenly a shining automobile swept toward her, and in a panic she picked up her suit case and started on again. Suppose it should be her future employer riding in that car! She did not want to be caught like a little tramp sitting on her dusty suit case by the road side!

But the car swept in at the drive after a pause for the chauffeur to open the gates, and she caught a glimpse of a proud woman and a girl with bright hair and reddened lips sitting in the tonneau.

By this time she was very tired and much disheartened. But there was only one more estate before she came to her destination so she took courage and plodded on. After all she wouldn't have thought this much of a walk if she had been at home. She couldn't have come more than three miles and what were three miles, even with a burden to carry? What was a mere little suit case? She had often carried heavier burdens, as far. No, it was her heavy heart that was the matter! She was homesick! Just plain homesick. She wanted to turn tail and run back where she had come from. She wanted to sit down to supper with Aunt Jocelyn and tell her about the journey. She wanted to eat the white raised biscuits and honey, and the dainty omelette Aunt Jocclyn would prepare. Oh, she was *hungry!* Just tired and hungry like a baby! She wanted to go to prayer mecting tonight and see if the boys of her Sunday School class would all be there. She wanted to play the wheezy old piano as she had done ever since she was a little girl; to hear the minister pray tenderly, as he would to-night she was sure, for "the one who has left us for a little while to do Thy will in other fields"— That would be the way he would put it. How it choked her to think about it all. How dear home seemed! Even the threadbare old red carpet in the prayer meeting room seemed dear, though there had been times in the past when she had hated it and longed to do something about getting a new one.

She wanted to be home and feel she had a right to stay there. Why, even Fred Holley's freckled face, and kindly smile would have been a welcome sight on that road at that minute, and if Fred Holley had only dreamed it possible he would have been there if he missed a whole day's work in his garage where he was doing so well; for Fred Holley had dogged her steps, and surrounded her with his unwelcome attentions ever since she was in High School, and he had been the one thing at home from which she was glad to get away.

She was plodding now past a long stretch of towering rhododendron that completely hid the second estate from the view of the road. It seemed endless, but on the other hand the scene was growing interesting. To the left of the road the land swept away into velvety billows and she presently became aware that she was passing a most marvelous golf course. Rayport had a golf club, and a fairly good course. She had often played on it with friends who were members, although she could not afford either the time or the money to join the country club herself. But she knew a golf course when she saw it, and by some fine instinct she became aware that this must be the most super golf course that her imagination had ever dreamed of.

A widely spreading, stately edifice presently came to view, nestled far among picturesque foliage, and this of course must be the country club. Likely they called it Briarcliff Country Club or else some fantastic more distinctive name. So she whiled her long pilgrimage with imaginings, and wondered if she would ever have opportunity to see that beautiful buiding nearer by.

Behind and beyond the country club buildings the valley stretched away to far reaches, like an endless golf course, and edging it were lovely hills, blending into blue distances. It was a sightly place in which she was walking. There was probably a marvelous view from those well hidden mansions behind the stone walls and thick rhododendron growth. And what would the third mansion be like where she was to abide for a time?

At last she came to a huge fence, like wrought-iron lace work, towering above her head, and behind it the soft feathery fringe of a beautiful hemlock hedge. It cast a cool shade along the road, and its breath seemed to fill the air with balm. It reminded her of the woods behind the old saw mill at home, and her step quickened eagerly.

The hedge with its iron enclosure reached farther than any of the other estate boundaries she had passed, but at last she came to an opening, hidden, almost disguised by the thick growth of great trees, which had been increasing the farther she went until now it seemed almost like a forest. Here suddenly the drive swept in by a cool dark curve into dense shade.

She stopped and caught her breath in delight. The sun was hot and she was very warm and tired. It was like a cooling breath, this lovely shaded way.

She entered, cautiously, like Alice going into Wonderland. It seemed unbelievable that she should be entering a place like this and presuming to think she belonged there. Could it be possible that this was the place where she was to spend the summer?

She sat down on her suit case again and taking off her hat let the breeze fan her heated forehead. She leaned back and looked up at the cool interlacing branches overhead, and drew in a deep breath of the resinous fragrance. Then with quick memory of the car that had swept into that other entrance farther back, she smoothed her hair and hastily put on her hat again, straightening it by the little mirror of her handbag. Some one might drive in here any minute and she would not wish to be caught this way even by a servant.

Then with renewed courage she took up her suit case and went on with brisker step up the drive.

Even then it was a good quarter of a mile before

she reached the house. The lovely winding drive went for a long distance, cool and deep among the pines and hemlocks, until she began to think she had made a mistake and gone into a forest instead of a gentleman's driveway. Then just as she was beginning to get anxious the foliage thinned, and there came a glimpse of a wonderful stone mansion like a crown upon the top of a rise of ground. She caught her breath, in wonder, this time exclaiming aloud. Could this be one man's house? A mansion indeed! It was like a castle! It could not be that this was the place where she was engaged to serve as secretary! She had somehow made a great mistake, come too far or something. But at least, now she had come she would go up to that mansion and see it. She could have the excuse that she had missed her way, and once, just once in a lifetime she would see what a great castle looked like close at hand.

She had some thought of leaving her suit case back under the bushes till she should return. It would be safe enough hidden under some of those low hanging hemlocks, and it would be so much easier walking, and so much more dignified than appearing at the door of a place like that to ask the way, lumbered up with a great shabby suit case.

Then she reflected that something might happen to her suit case, some dog pull it apart, or a tramp find it, and she could not afford to lose her meager wardrobe. So she toiled on.

But the way grew lovelier as she neared the house. Fountains were revealed in nooks by the way, dripping cool from the rocky crevice of a little unsuspected grotto into a great stone jar that reminded one of Old Testament wells and shepherd girls; or showering soft silver spray into a quiet pool where lazy lilies rested and silent goldfish glided like brilliant phantasms beneath the surface. And higher up in the sunlight there were great bursts of flowers, like broidery in borders on the lawns and fringing the terraces. More than once she stopped in ecstasy over the beauty opening out before her, and still the castle seemed remote.

The drive wound out at last and suddenly the mansion stood before her close at hand, and seemed almost overaweing in its grandeur. Built of rough stone in severe but classic lines, it seemed like some great rock that had not been made with hands. Its battlements clear cut against the bright afternoon sky were startling. She could scarcely believe that she was standing so near to anything that looked so like a picture from the old world, so much a thing of history and of the past. Of course it was a reproduction of some great old historic wonder. Nothing modern could be so perfect and so much a thing that seemed to have stood through the ages.

A stone seat withdrawn from the edge of the drive into a shelter of sweeping trees offered harbor while she took breath and gathered courage, and she dropped upon it and gazed; gradually turning her eyes from the house itself to the view across the great lawn, and down the valley. And now she saw that she had climbed far above the tall hemlocks that fringed the road so thickly, and could look across them, to the hills beyond. The country club seemed a mere toy in the distance from this point. A wonderful view, with a silver river winding in the valley like a plaything! One could not think of even a mansion in the sky having any more wonderful view.

The sound of an approaching motor brought her back to her own situation once more, and she arose hastily and hurried toward what appeared to be the main entrance of the house wondering if perhaps she ought not to hunt a door more fitting for a mere secretary's entrance.

An imposing butler answered her timid ring, and when she said, "I'm Miss Lorrimer," he said, "Oh, yes, Miss Lorrimer. The maid will show you to your room."

Amory had a glimpse of space and beauty, soft colors and abundant ease, a suggestion of lovely things in their rightful settings such as she had read about and dreamed about but never hoped to see with her earthly eyes.

The maid appeared like a genii and led her up wide stairs and down a corridor that gave upon the room below in many little latticed windows. She had a glimpse of lovely rooms done in soft pastel colorings, of silken draperies, priceless rugs, and luxury everywhere. Then a door was thrown open into a room done in cool pale green and silver, with wide windows, low seats, and a couch and desk that were attractive.

The maid opened another door and Amory saw another smaller room, with rosy draperies on the bed and at the windows and glimpsed a white tiled bath through the door beyond.

"Madam thought you could be comfortable here," said the maid in a colorless voice, "she wanted you near her own apartments for convenience in the mornings."

"Oh, it is lovely!" said Amory with her heart in her eyes, and then remembered that she must not gush before servants, and that she must not behave as if she were not used to nice things; two of the principles in which she had been trying to school herself ever since she received the letter saying her application had been accepted.

"Thank you," she said less eagerly, with a lovely smile to the other young woman, "I am sure I shall be quite comfortable here. And now, I wonder if you can tell me when I can see Mrs. Whitney."

"To-morrow morning," said the maid still color-lessly, "Madam has a house party on and the place is full of guests. She'll be busy all the afternoon and evening, but she'll see you at ten to-morrow. She'll ring for you then, and I'll show you the way to her room. She said you'd want to rest and get settled. Has your luggage come yet? Did you bring it in the taxi with you?"

Amory grew pink remembering her long walk, and the precious dollar she had saved; conscious too of her dusty slippers. But she must not tell the servant that she had walked. She must remember those things. And of course she should have known that it was no way to arrive at a place like this, on foot and carrying her own suit case! However she would prob-ably learn.

"They are sending my trunk from the station soon," she said walking over toward the window and trying to look unflustered. And then catching sight of the view from the window she forgot her resolve about gushing and burst forth again with a soft ex-clamation:

"Oh, isn't it lovely from the window!" she said, as if the maid were another girl like herself, "I shall just drink in all this beauty!"

"Yes, it's a sightly place," said the girl as if such things mattered little to her. "Would you like me to unpack your suit case for you? Madam said I was to help you in any way you needed—."

Amory turned and flashed another smile at her.

"Oh, no, please," she said with an inward gasp at the idea of this prim maid going over all her intimate little economies, and pitiful make-shifts. "I've nothing else to do, you know, and I'll enjoy getting settled."

"Very well," said the colorless voice. "Then I'll go down. It's time to serve tea, and they'll be wanting me. I'll bring your tea up here."

"Oh!" said Amory, quite wondering at the idea, for tea wasn't served as a rule in Rayport unless one was giving an affair. But she realized that she was hungry and tea would be very refreshing.

"But, do you need to bother coming up? Couldn't I just slip down and get it myself, if you would show me the way about?"

"It's no trouble," said the maid and Amory couldn't be sure whether there was a note of scorn in her voice for one who had offered to serve herself, or whether it was gratitude.

"I'll show you about later, if you like," added the maid and going out, closed the door.

Suddenly Amory felt tremendously alone, shut in by walls so thick that no sound penetrated, surrounded by a loveliness that was so foreign to all that she had known before that it made her throat ache to look at it. She felt as if she had stolen, unaware to the owners, into a spot that was too great for her small powers. She ought to go down, and find them, somewhere, somehow, and tell them that she was only a bluff and that she would never be able to fill any kind of a position in such a great house as this.

But here she was, and bidden to keep out of the way till the morrow. There was nothing to do but put her things neatly away and bide her time until summoned to her employer.

She went about the room examining every article, and making soft little gleeful noises of pleasure over things. This room was no servant's quarters. It had evidently been one of the regular guest rooms, for everything in it was beautiful.

She went into the rose draped bedroom and looked around in delight. She flung open a door that she thought must be a closet and a light sprang forth, revealing a room as large as Aunt Hannah's bedroom in Rayport. Rods and hangers and shelves! Shoes trees and hat trees galore! Surely the maid had made a dreadful mistake and put her in the wrong room. Perhaps she ought to do something about it.

She hung up her small dark hat on a hand painted dolly. She hung up her limp little georgette coat in which she had journeyed on a pink satin hanger finished in rosebuds. Then she went into the spacious white bathroom finished in rose and black borders, and washed her face and hands with a cake of soap that she had seen much advertised in the magazines, but had never hoped to use because of its price. If this room was a mistake at least she would have this few minutes of the fun of playing it belonged to her.

When she had made her hair smooth and tidy, and had hung up one or two things out of her suit case that she was afraid might muss she went and sat down by the window in her green sitting room.

"This is my boudoir!" she said to herself looking around with shining eyes. "What fun I'll have writing to Aunt Hannah and Aunt Jocelyn about it!"

Then her eyes sought the lovely distance.

And all at once she saw something like a bird, or perhaps it was only a large insect sailing across the sky. Of course it was an airplane, but what fun to watch it from such a high place! She never had been where she could watch one so well. They were always high up overhead when they went over Rayport.

The insect became a bird, and the bird a great

plane at last, flashing its silver wings in the sunlight. She knelt by the window sill and looked up at it. It seemed to be coming straight toward the house, and she could hear the throb of the engine now. Was that the flier looking down? It thrilled her to think she was so near to the great machine, and to the man who dared to navigate the skies.

Then down below she heard voices, gay, laughing, and a group of young people suddenly appeared on the terrace in light lovely dresses, sport frocks and flannels, things she had read about. They were looking up and calling, waving their hands. One girl took the long coral scarf from her head and waved it.

"That's Teddy!" they called, "There he is! I knew he'd be on time!"

A white paper fluttered down as the plane circled away, and the girls ran screaming and laughing to catch it.

"It's mine!" they called.

"No! It's mine!"

"Better give it to Diana!" some one laughed. "She claims all that flies as her own!"

Amory drew back into the shadow of the curtain lest she might be seen by the gay crowd below, but her eyes were on the great plane which was circling lower and lower now, and she realized with another thrill that it was going to land right there and she was going to be able to see it.

The flying field was not a quarter of a mile away, just beyond the garden, and the hedge was low there. Amory was far above the ground, and felt that she had a front seat at the most exciting moment of her life.

Like a great silver moth it settled down, ran smoothly for a little space and came to rest. She watched it in wonder, and presently a figure disengaged himself from the body of the machine and after walking about the creature and examining it here and there started toward the garden gate.

As he came nearer Amory could see that he wore an aviator's costume, and that he had a goodly countenance, tanned to a lovely golden brown.

Striding through the garden gate as the troup of young people ran laughing to meet him, he pulled off his helmet and swung it in his hand. She saw that he had golden brown hair, crisp and curly, and short cut, and a strong well chiseled chin and nose. His eyes were very blue, and he raised them suddenly to her window, while the group of giddy girls below caught him, and pulled him and pretended to try to kiss him. They were laughing eyes, and they looked straight into Amory's, who had forgotten to stay in the shadow, with a laughing astonished question in their blue depths.

"What does he see? What is he looking at?" cried the struggling girls as he warded them off, and they all looked up at Amory's window, but Amory was not there. She had dropped suddenly to her knees with her burning cheeks hidden in her hands.

And just then there came a knock at the door!

CHAPTER II

IT was only the maid with a tray, but Amory was trembling as if she were about to be brought to trial in a court of law. What on earth was the matter with her, she wondered, acting silly like this! Just because she had been caught looking out of the window. She had a right to look out of the window didn't she, even if she was only a hired secretary?

She scrambled to her feet and met the question in the maid's eye.

"I was watching an airplane land," she explained confusedly.

"Oh, that's Mr. Theodore," explained the maid. "He's just back from his Canada hop. They said he was coming but his aunt didn't seem to expect him very much. Now he's come things will happen fast. He keeps things always on the go."

"Oh," said Amory striving for some of her vanished dignity. "Does he live here? It must be exciting to have some one you know flying."

"Well, no, he doesn't live here, but he comes often. His aunt always sends for him whenever she has a house party. But since he's been flying she can't always get him. That's why she let them make a flying field over there on her property, so he could come just any time and not have to travel far after he landed. Do you like your tea strong, Miss Lorrimer? And will you have cream or lemon."

"Oh, lemon, please," said Amory, "but don't trouble about me. I'll look after myself. I'm used to doing it."

"You're very kind," said the maid, "but I have my orders of course. The cook sent you a bit of salad, and a chicken sandwich. She thought you might be hungry after your journey, and dinner's not till half past eight."

"Oh, that was kind," said Amory. "Thank her for me, please. And I hope I can do something for both of you sometime."

The maid melted a little from her settled apathy.

"You can call me Christine," she volunteered, "and I'll be back later for the tray."

The tray proved to be most tempting. Delicate little chicken sandwiches, a delectable salad of which Amory had difficulty in identifying the ingredients, fragrant tea, cinnamon toast and little cakes that were almost confections.

She settled down in a discreet chair quite out of range from any curious eyes below, and arranged the curtain so that she could watch the pretty panorama, bright costumes on the terrace, and listen to the gay banter as it rose to her window, while she ate.

Several young men had appeared below, and there was a subdued clatter of tea things as the well trained servants moved about serving everybody. Amory could see Christine waiting with her serving tray, and that would likely be Mrs. Whitney in the heliotrope frock pouring the tea. Amory felt she was wearing far too startling a make-up to be pleasant, for the contrast of her whitened skin, carmine lips and dead black severely cut hair did not make a pleasing ensemble. Yet she could see that there was a certain style and character about her that made her attractive. She noticed that all listened when she spoke as if they liked her and wanted to please her.

The Whitney girls were probably those two with dark hair and blue eyes. They looked like their mother, and presently she heard some one say, "Caroline Whitney, where on earth have you been all the afternoon? You don't mean you went off and played tennis again with that kid brother of yours! I say that isn't fair. None of the rest of us are practicing for the tournament."

"Oh," said the girl called Caroline, "you all have the same opportunity to practice. There are plenty of courts and Ned will play with anybody that asks him at any hour of the day."

"I'll say he will," said the other dark girl. "He's nagged me all day long, but I couldn't see it. It was too hot."

So, she had identified three of the household. Now who was the striking girl with the gold hair? Beautiful even in spite of the dangling earrings, and the too high color which to Amory seemed in bad taste. Stay! wasn't she the one who had caught the fluttering paper from the airplane as if it were her right? She must be Diana then.

And now came the young aviator, with marvelous promptness considering that he seemed to have changed his garments and looked as fresh as if he had not just arrived from a long flight.

It was interesting to watch them as they sat chatting and sipping their tea, calling little nothings back and forth to one another, gossiping about others who were to arrive that evening or on the morrow. Amory from her sheltered chair behind the curtain could see them all quite well, and hear what they were saying. She hoped it wasn't eavesdropping, this watching in on a group of beings who were as much out of her world as a bird is out of a human's universe. It was just as well, she thought, for her to get a line on the people she was to be among. It would help her to adjust her life to her surroundings more quickly.

She sat there after she had finished her tray and put it aside, trying to think how it would seem if she were one of the guests in that house, instead of a paid secretary. How would she feel if she were sitting, for instance, down in that great chair with the high fan-shaped back, where the golden Diana sat, and the young aviator near with his teacup in his hand looking down and smiling at her? Would she be able to hold her own in a group of young people like that? It was not her world, but could she make a good showing in it if she had to, or would she be shy and awkward and be thinking of herself all the time?

But what a silly idea. It was not her world and why should she imagine such things?

She was half impatiently turning away from the window when Mrs. Whitney spoke, and she lingered to listen to the pleasant cultured voice, curious to know just what her employer would be like.

"I have just had a most annoying letter from Mr. Whitney's nephew," she said in a voice touched just the least shade with plaintiveness, as if appealing to her young guests to somehow make right whatever was troubling her. "He writes that he is coming on to visit us if we will have him, and of course Mr. Whitney will think he'll have to be made welcome. The worst of it is Mr. Whitney adores him. He's the son of his youngest sister who died years ago, and he's idealized her. I shall have to have him, there are no two ways about it."

Groans ensued from the two young Whitney girls. "What a plague!" said Caroline tossing her curly black mane.

"It's perfectly poisonous!" said Doris. "I mean to reason with Dad about it."

"Well, it won't do a particle of good!" said the mother sweetly. "Besides, he's on the way. He'll be here to-morrow morning, more is the pity, and your father won't be at home till to-morrow night. If I should tell him we had no room for his only nephew he would never forgive me."

"What's the matter with him? Why worry so much? Isn't he young?" called out a young woman who was stretched with a good length of silk stocking in evidence, on a long steamer chair. "Let him come! We can get away with several more men in the crowd and not know it."

"Oh, but Susanne, he's quite impossible!" said the hostess wearily. "He's religious you know and he wouldn't be in the least congenial. In fact he's a regular preacher, has taken some kind of orders, you know. Besides all that, he holds some awfully queer ideas. Thinks the end of the world is coming soon or something like that. Oh, he's quite impossible! And to have him arrive just at this time too when I wanted everything to be perfect!"

"Holy Cats!" exclaimed an impudent pink cheeked girl whose body resembled an animated lath, "I should say! Mother Whitney, what'll you give us if we get rid of him without bothering Papa Whitney at all? I'll bet we could do it. Leave it to us, and we'll send him flying without letting him know what it's all about."

"That's an idea!" said one of the young men. "Send him flying! Get Teddy to carry him off and lose him, somewhere so far away he can't get back till the party's over."

"Oh, but Mr. Whitney would never forgive Ted if he did that. Besides, I doubt if John would go. He's quite too devoted to his work to take a day off for anything he considers worldly. I don't know how he is now, but he was bad enough as a child. He's bound to be worse from all I've heard."

"Well, it will be dead easy to get rid of him," declared Susanne. "We'll just whoop it up and make it too hot for him to stay! He'll pick up his effects and run, if he's that kind. I personally will see to that."

"But, Susanne dear," pleaded the hostess, "I couldn't really let you do that, for the man will simply have to stay until his engagement to preach is over. It seems he's supplying the village church for three weeks, and Mr. Whitney will insist on our being courteous to him. I'm not sure but he will think we ought to even go to church to hear him."

Groans ensued from the entire party, and then Diana spoke up.

"What's the use in making such a fuss about something we can't help? Leave him to me! I'll make him forget he's ever seen a pulpit! Let's make the best of it and get a good time out of it. What do you say to my getting the poor simp to fall for me and reducing him to common sense? I think it would be rather fun myself. I'm tired to death of all the old excitements and would just enjoy a new thrill."

"Mercy, Diana, he wouldn't look at you, with all that make-up on you!" declared his cousin Caroline with a sneer. "Why, he'd simply run from the sight of those worldly earrings, and you'd have to let down your skirts and wear stockings! I'm sure if he would ever see you in your new bathing suit he'd faint completely away, and you wouldn't have a chance with him unless you cut all cocktails and stopped smoking!"

"It couldn't be did!" chanted the cousin Doris. "Even Diana couldn't do that!"

"Oh, yes, I could if I chose," said Diana lazily looking up at the clouds. "I'm not sure but I'd enjoy it. I could get converted you know. It would be a new line. Ingénue you know. I could telephone in town for some simple white frocks. If I couldn't get rid of him I could at least keep him busy so he wouldn't bother the rest of you."

"Oh, but really, Diana, I couldn't let a guest sacrifice herself to that extent. I really couldn't," protested the hostess.

"But it wouldn't be sacrifice," said Diana showing her pretty white teeth in a fiendish little grin. "I tell you it would be a new thrill, and I'll do it so perfectly that Papa Whitney will never suspect."

"But Diana, I wouldn't like to have you carry it too far! You know Mr. Whitney was very fond of his youngest sister—and the young man is really a fine fellow, only he just doesn't fit here—"

"I understand, Mamma Whitney, and I won't be anything but a means of grace to the dear fellow— isn't that what you call it? I'll just let him see how much he's missing, being like that. That's all."

Mrs. Whitney smiled indulgently at the pretty girl and shook her head reprovingly.

"Oh, Di, Di, I'm afraid you are incorrigible. You're just like your mother when she was your age! Well, I'll have to leave you to your fun of course, only I do hope you'll be discreet. You know you can carry even a joke too far, and I shouldn't like my nephew to think we were rude to him. Because of course he is a relative."

"Do you really mean it, Diana?" asked Caroline sitting up from her recumbent position on the terrace. "What will you do if Barry Blaine gets here? You can't play too parts at once."

"Well, you may have him, darling Caroline, just for the occasion you know. I know you'll be fair about it, and I'd rather you had him than any of the other girls because you won't take too much advantage of me."

This remark was answered with screams of laughter from the rest of the group.

"Well, you'd better go in, Diana, and get your make-up off, if you really mean it," called Caroline who had been looking over her mother's shoulder and reading her cousin's letter, "for he'll never look at you like that. I imagine it'll take you some time to make up for your new part. I doubt if you can do it first off."

"Thanks!" said Diana lazily, "leave my part to me. I don't intend to take off anything for the first act, please, he's got to take an interest in me, see, and try to convert me, because I'm so worldly. Don't worry, I've got it all thought out."

"And where do I come in?" asked the aviator hanging over Diana's chair and laughing down into her eyes.

"Oh, you come in for the first dance to-morrow night, old Teddy. We'll do the latest for him, and let him see how worldly I am right at the start, see?"

"My eye, you will!" said Caroline. "*He'll* not be there. John never was known to go to a dance, and he'll run from the house the minute it's mentioned. You see!"

"He'll be *there!*" said Diana, prettily confident, "and he'll *see* me! You wait and watch, infant! There are more ways than one of catching a fly, and you don't know them all yet. Come on, Susanne, I'm going up and take a nap to be bright and fresh for the evening unless"—and she lingered looking up at the young aviator, "unless Teddy's game for a set of tennis before he dresses."

"Sold!" said the aviator, and catching her hand he ran off to the tennis court.

Laughing, the rest of the company broke up, and scattered into the house.

The two Whitney girls lingered to speak annoyedly to their mother.

"Well, I don't think Diana will do anything really rude, dear," said the mother. "You know she can always get around Daddy! Yes, I understand that this is quite a crowd to handle, but I don't really think any of them will overstep the mark. And anyhow I had to explain him somehow before he came. Now, girls, run and get a little rest before dinner. You both have dark circles under your eyes, and it isn't becoming. Your father'll notice it pretty soon, and that'll not be so good."

The terrace grew quiet and Amory came out from her hiding and peered down below. The sun was dropping low toward a mountain in the distance and casting long shadows of the trees on the lawn. There was a rosy light over everything, and the world looked very beautiful and good. Yet the girl as she stood there looking down at the deserted chairs pushed back and the littered tea table, suddenly shivered as she thought over what she had just heard.

Was it possible they all meant that cruel joke? Were they really going to play a farce on a poor young fellow who was probably from the country somewhere and would not understand what was being done to him? Would they really carry it out, or were they just joking among themselves? She could not think that anybody would be so mean.

She thought back to the time when Hiram Rice had decided to go as a missionary, and their little church in Rayport had raised the money to send him, all their own, their first missionary. Of course he couldn't speak correct English, and he had never studied Greek nor Hebrew, but his heart was on fire with love for God, and his face was radiant at the thought of going off to Africa and enduring privations for the sake of being used to spread the gospel. Hiram Rice was homely and uncouth in some ways. His hands were big and red and his face had a way of turning purple when a lady spoke to him, but he was sincere and earnest as the day is long, and even if he did pray with a louder tone than he needed to use to reach the throne of heaven, there was not a soul in Rayport who would have made fun of him. They were all proud of him.

This cousin who was so unwelcome might be even more peculiar and uninteresting than Hiram Rice, yet it seemed a terrible thing to Amory that any set of young people should deliberately set out to make fun of and disturb his peace of mind! Her soul arose in indignation against them all. Mrs. Whitney, too, had seemed to be lenient with the idea, had almost encouraged it; at least she had not forbidden it, and it was all too evident that she could have done so if she chose. What a set of people! To have all that these people had, a house like this, a palace set on a hill where they could see the very kingdoms of the earth; all that money could buy; not a care in the world; and nothing to do but play! And yet they could not endure the presence of a relative who was not congenial to them for a few days! How she despised them all! Despised most of all the golden girl who was going to be the star actor in this despicable play they were planning for an unsuspecting victim.

Of course there was little likelihood that she would come into touch with any of the people who had entered into this remarkable plot for the unsettling of the young preacher, but there might be a chance sometime for her to give him a hint, to help him out somewhere, or even to quietly do something that would foil some of their schemes. If she could she certainly would. If anonymous letters were not so ill bred she might even bring herself to write him one and warn him.

Oh, well, of course it was none of her business! And she must be most careful for Aunt Hannah's dear sake that she did nothing to lose her job. She was not here to be a philanthropist. She was here to earn money to send home to the two dear women who had brought her up and cared for her all her life. She must not forget that!

She turned from her window and walked restlessly back around the room. And now the beautiful hangings, and the expensive trinkets with which the dressing table was strewn seemed almost hateful to her.

People who could afford luxuries and yet had no loving kindness in their hearts! People who had no reverence for the things of God! How did they dare talk
that way, lightly, about one who was giving his life
to preaching, no matter how fanatical he might be?
Well, of course she had not seen the cousin yet, but
somehow she could not help feeling indignant for
him.

Christine tapped at the door.

"It's your trunk, Miss Lorrimer," she said, "and
Madam says will you please be ready to come down
and take a place at the table in case you're needed.
One of the lady guests has not arrived yet, though
there's still another train she may come on in time
for dinner. The chauffeur has gone down to the station now, and I'll let you know if she comes. But
you'll please be dressed in case she does not get
here!"

When the trunk was unlocked and the door had
closed on man and maid Amory stood aghast in the
middle of her big new apartment and looked at her
little shabby trunk. What was there in that trunk
that could compete with the gay feathers those birds
of paradise who were guests in the house would
wear? What had she that would not be conspicuous
because of its simplicity? It had not occurred to her
that she would have social obligations as well as
clerical in this new situation.

She glanced at her watch to see how much time she
had, and then she went at unpacking her trunk,
thinking hard as she worked. There was a white
chiffon carefully folded lying in the top tray. She had
made it herself by a well selected pattern from
one of the best pattern houses in the world. Before
she packed it she had tried it on again and decided
that it would stand with anything the world could
produce as far as line and style went. The material

was sheer and soft and becoming. It had a sweet round neck and a deep fall of drapery over the shoulder because Aunt Hannah did not like ordinary evening dress, did not think it modest. It had been carefully picoted at the village shop by loving hands, and cut with utmost scrupulous pains by Aunt Jocelyn afterwards. There was a short string of imitation pearls to wear with it, and as raiment it had seemed to her when she packed it that heart could desire no more.

Yet now, after this one short hour of watching those idle rich girls at their tea, she knew in her heart that this her finest robe would look no more the proper thing for a dinner gown at the Whitney's house party than if she went down in the dark little crepe she was wearing now.

She reviewed her few other dresses. A light blue voile, and a pink crepe de chine, dyed with a ten cent dye in the wash bowl, and made up new. Both had a homemade look, she knew.

Well, it would have to be the white dress of course. She had known it all along, but she trembled as she put it over her head and arranged the sweet drapery about her shoulders. They would think she was a little grammar school girl wearing her commencement frock. Why hadn't she known that before she left home? How did she find it out in that one brief hour of watching the other girls?

Well, and what could she have done about it if she had found out? There was no money to buy more new dresses. They had strained a point and let the grocery bill go unpaid for a whole month to get that one for her. She must make this job pay at least long enough to pay back for that dress.

There were new white slippers to go with it, that was a comfort. Of course the others would wear gold and silver, she knew that now. She had read fashion magazines enough to understand what people like these people wore and did; her only trouble had been in not placing her employer in the right stratum of social life.

She was dressed and waiting when Christine tapped at the door, and she looked very lovely. The maid gave her an approving glance sitting by the table where the silk shade cast rosy lights upon her white neck and the little cheap string of pearls. Something in Christine's glance gave Amory more courage as she rose to follow the maid.

"It's a pity," said Christine, eyeing with approval the slim white figure, the trim slippers, and the pretty brown head with its natural waves. "It's a pity, Miss Lorrimer, now you've gone to all that trouble, but she's come! She just arrived this minute. I'm bringing your dinner up and Mrs. Whitney said there were books in the book case if you like to read. But maybe you'd like to go out a bit in the twilight after you've eaten. There'll be nobody about for a good full hour and a half, and it's lovely with the full moon to-night."

So Amory ate her solitary meal in the big green room with the pink light off behind the mountains where the sun had set, and the soft blue light of the moon beginning to steal faintly over the landscape that lay like a picture out of her window.

There came a lump in her throat as she thought of the pleasant supper table at home, with Aunt Jocelyn sitting alone to-night eating a solitary supper too, and leaving the door open into Aunt Hannah's bedroom for company, for the new nurse would not arrive until to-morrow.

Later, she followed Christine's directions and stole down a back stairway between the servants' quarters and the main part of the house, and so at last stood out upon the terrace with its tall backed wicker chairs, and its wonderful outlook upon a world now bathed in soft moonlight.

For a moment she dropped down softly into the great chair where Diana Dorne had sat and feasted her eyes upon the beauty of the night. Then quietly she arose and stole softly about on the terrace, looking the house over from every possible angle. How beautiful and satisfying her castle was in every line and turret! It was just as she would have it if she were able to build one for herself!

When she came to the side of the house where the dining room windows looked out, she stole farther away upon the lawn and looked in from afar. But she need not have worried, for the people were eating and drinking and thinking of nothing outside the four walls of that spacious room, and she moved on without having been noticed.

There was plenty of time for she had seen the butler bringing in the salad plates, so she went for a stroll down the lawn, and came at last to the little garden gate that opened into the flying field.

Curiously she looked over. There lay the great plane all quiet in the moonlight, like a sleeping monster, the silver of its wings gleaming softly.

She looked about her cautiously. There was still the subdued distant clatter of silver and crystal and china, and a faint murmur of voices all talking at once, two choruses, one from the dining room, the other from the kitchen quarters.

What harm to go over there and look at that plane? There seemed to be no one about even to guard it.

She swung the gate open and stepped into the field, going swiftly over to where the plane lay, with a feeling that she was a naughty little girl about to do some terrible forbidden thing. But she did so want to see how a real airplane looked close by. That would be something to write to Aunt Hannah about, and she might never have such another good chance when nobody was by.

She walked all about it and surveyed it, and grew quite familiar with its lines, studied on her tip toes the cockpit and engine, noted the seat for the driver, and passengers, the various gauges and levers that must work the curious mechanism of the great bird. Then she drew a deep sigh of wonder and looked up into the clear sky with the moon sailing high, and her young heart thrilled at the sight. After all the moon was greater than any airplane, and the moon had been with the earth for ages.

"Oh!" she breathed softly, "Oh!" like a prayer, and turned about to face toward the house for it was growing late and was time to go in if she would be out of sight before any one came out.

"Oh, I say!" said a voice so near to her ear that it made her jump, "are you real, or a spirit? I wasn't quite sure, though I tell you the truth I haven't been drinking."

She laughed out softly for relief. She knew at once who it was the aviator, and she didn't feel afraid. Of all the people she had seen down on the terrace she felt the least afraid of him.

"Oh, I'm real," she gurgled, dizzily, "but I didn't mean to stay so long. I just wanted to see how it looked close by. Do you mind? I didn't touch anything."

"Mind? Why should I mind? Bless your heart, I'm glad you're real. You got my goat I'll confess, back there a minute ago. I've been on a stiff trip, and I thought I must be going fluey. Who are you anyway? I haven't met you have I? Are you one of our house guests, or do you come from the neighbors?"

"I'm nobody!" said Amory hastily, "I'm just the new secretary. I haven't seen anybody yet. I'm to see Mrs. Whitney in the morning."

"For sweet pity's sake, girl! And they've kept a jewel like you hidden out of sight all this time. I'll tell my aunt what she's done. Come on in. You haven't had a bite to eat I'll warrant."

"Oh yes I have!" protested Amory hastily, "I've had my dinner. I preferred to be by myself to-night. Really, please don't—!" she ended in a panic as he seized her arm and seemed about to walk her into the house.

"Do you honestly mean it?" he demanded looking down at her earnestly. "Well then I won't. It's nicer out here anyway. How would you like to take a little fly with me? It's a perfect night."

"Oh, I couldn't, thank you!" said Amory appalled and shrinking away. "I really must go into the house at once. I have things that I must do—I really!— You mustn't— Please!"

It was a different kind of tone from the way the girls he knew protested against his attentions. Their protest he knew was not genuine. This bore panic in it, and reached his heart.

"Well, see here now, I won't bother you if you feel that way, but I want to show you my plane. You're interested in it, aren't you? Well, then why shouldn't I show it to you? You aren't in such a doggone hurry, are you? I'm perfectly respectable."

"Oh, I know," she laughed, "you're Mrs. Whitney's nephew. But I'm only the secretary, and I shouldn't be out here. I'm sure you understand."

"Well, all right!" said the hearty young voice unconvincedly. "When will you come then? How about to-morrow morning early? Since we've been introduced just now we aren't of course strangers any more and by to-morrow morning we'll be old friends you know. There won't a soul of them be up before nine o'clock anyway after this shindig to-night. What if you were to come for a walk say at seven to-morrow morning and step over here from the garden. I'm hopping off about seven thirty for a spin to New York. I may be back in a few days and I may not. You never can tell, and I've got a hunch I'd like to show you my boat before I go. No, they don't know I'm going and I'm not going to tell them, and if you don't come down and see me set sail I'll have to start off all alone without anybody to wish me good luck. Will you come?"

She smiled at him wistfully in the moonlight.

"Why, I'll wish you good luck—" she said shyly, "or better, I'll pray you safe return."

"That's the talk," he said earnestly. "I never had any one promise to do that, but I have a hunch it might do some good if you did it. And now, will you come down and see me start off? I'd like to show you how the thing goes. She's a good old bird. Will you come?"

"Perhaps!" said Amory softly, "I'll think about it," and she turned and fled to the house.

CHAPTER III

At first when Amory awoke in the morning she could not remember where she was, but gradually as she looked about on her rose-hung chamber it all came back. She was a secretary in a mansion on a hill, and a bird man with a kindly face and a hearty voice was waiting for her to see him take off from the field outside the garden gate.

Of course she would not go down. Aunt Hannah and Aunt Jocelyn would be scandalized at the idea. And yet, would they? They would be interested themselves to see a plane and watch it start from earth. Was there anything wrong in her being out there and letting him show her what made the great bird rise and soar?

She argued it out with herself again and again, always coming back to the same decision that she must not go, yet something drew her continually. After all, why was it wrong? She would likely never see him again, and in any other situation in life she would have stopped to watch, even to ask questions of a stranger about a great wonder like a plane.

She was so deep in her thoughts that she forgot the wonders of her luxurious bath room, and took her shower as unconcernedly as if she had had a silver mounted one opening out of her room every day since she was born.

She put on a plain little cotton gown with blue flowers trailing over it and cute pockets and a belt. The blue of the flowers took its color from her eyes, or vice versa.

And when she was dressed she knelt down by her bed and prayed. Then she put her little Testament in one of the cute pockets and slipped out of her door softly down the stairs.

The morning was fresh and sweet, and she walked all around the house again seeing how it looked by daylight, and taking in its goodly battlements. She walked through the garden too, stopping to smell the roses, and to watch a bee take his fill of honey, and then she dropped down on a stone bench half hidden by great lilac bushes, and took out her little Testament. The bench was not a great way from the garden gate, and when the plane started, *if* it really started, for she had her suspicions that perhaps he was only jesting with her, she would slip to the garden gate and watch it ride away. There would be no harm in that and he likely wouldn't see her at all.

So she watched the house from her lilac covert, and read her Testament quietly. No one came out, and the house was still. There was no sound as yet even from the servants' quarters.

The dew of the morning was on all the flowers about her and the sweetness of their fragrance was in the air. She drew deep breaths of it, and wondered how she could put it all on paper for Aunt Hannah. Somehow she must manage to convey the breath of the morning and the pearl in the mist on the mountains so that Aunt Hannah could see and smell it.

It was just then that the voice spoke behind her:

"So you did come after all. I knew you would. I was sure you wouldn't fail me."

"Oh, but I didn't; I wasn't!" she breathed in consternation. "I'm just here—" she began to try to explain.

"Yes, you didn't but you did!" he insisted with his pleasant grin as he appeared around the lilacs dressed in his flying togs. "I say, anyway, you're here, and that's the important thing. What are you presumably doing?"

"Just reading," said Amory, closing her Testament and slipping it into her pocket. "I thought if you did fly I'd like to see you start," she explained shyly.

"You mean you meant to see me but you didn't intend I should see you. Is that it? Well, I'm not sure that's quite fair, but I'll take the will for the deed. However, now you're here I intend to show you my bird. There really is no point to your not looking it over now we are both here, and it is broad daylight. Come on."

He reached out a hand and grasped hers, bringing her to her feet and she had no choice but to follow unless she wished to make a scene. Embarrassed she hastened her steps, anxious to get quickly beyond the garden gate and out of sight of the house.

"Now," said he, dropping her hand as they approached the plane, "I'll show you first how the engine works. Suppose you get in. I can show you better from inside."

"Oh, no!" she said shrinking back.

"You don't trust me," he said gravely looking down with sudden challenge in his eyes. "You think I would run away with you against your will. But— I'm a gentleman, truly— At least I try to be."

"No!" she protested, a flood of color in her face, "I didn't think that! I'm sure you would not do anything like that. But I would not like anybody from the house to see me in there. It might be very much misunderstood."

"I see," said the young man pleasantly. "That's true too, but you must remember we are not strangers. I've met you before. I'll take the next opportunity, when I get back, to let that be known too, whether you are here or whether you are not here, so there'll be no chance of more misunderstandings."

"But—that's not quite true," she smiled, "we are strangers."

"No," said he solemnly, yet with a twinkle in his nice blue eyes, "you are quite mistaken. I met you out here last evening and we were formally introduced by yourself then, but of course I had really met you once before."

She looked at him startled, half puzzled.

"You don't remember? Why think! Weren't you looking out of a window when I came up on yonder terrace yesterday at tea time? And I looked straight into your eyes and you into mine, and we knew right then that we were friends, that we had been friends for a long time only we hadn't found each other. Isn't that so? It took me half the night thinking it over to locate your eyes, but when I remembered you looking out of that window I knew at once. Now, take that for what it's worth. When I get back I'm going to pursue this subject, but we haven't time now. We're friends. That's settled isn't it?"

She smiled assentingly in spite of inward qualms of conscience. Wasn't this just the kind of flirting that other girls did? The thing she had always despised so? But how could she help it without being prudish? Well, he would be gone in a minute and she would get back into the house and forget it. But he was nice and pleasant and not at all silly in the way he looked at her. Perhaps it was just his line of talk, and she would take it as that and not make a fuss.

"Now, we must get to work. I haven't much time. I ought to have been off an hour ago, but I wouldn't go till you came."

"Oh," she protested, "you shouldn't have waited. I'm sorry—"

"Yes, I'm sorry we haven't more time too," he smiled, "but we'll make a lot of what we have. Now, see this wheel—? See this lever?—?—"

He went forward with a rapid explanation of the mechanism of his machine. He took her around it and explained the principle of its going, and how it was made thus and so, and why; and then, as if it had been a lesson he was reciting rapidly because he had promised and wanted it over, he turned to her with a smile.

"Well, I've got to hop off," he said. "I'm due in New York before noon. When I come back will you take a spin with me?"

Amory looked troubled.

"You forget, I'm only here as a sort of—servant— in the house. I'm not here socially. I don't see how I could, thank you."

"But you'd not be afraid?"

"Oh, no, I'd love it. But I know it would not be expected of me." She looked into his eyes and he found a satisfying trust there that pleased him, for he answered it with his nice grin.

"All right sister! I'll fix that part so your conscience won't be hurt. Now, listen! There's a proposition on for me to make a trial trip to Siberia by way of Alaska. It's never been done and I think I can do it. Nobody here knows this, and I don't want it known till it comes off, *if* it comes off. But if it doesn't fall through I shan't come back here till I've made it. See? And I had a fancy I'd like you to know and wish me good luck. I knew when I looked into your eyes yesterday that you were one I could trust. You see now why I had to work fast, and be a little cavemannish about it don't you? You know I might not come back at all, sister, in which case you won't be the least little bit worse off than before. But I'd like your farewell good will if you don't mind."

Amory lifted eyes that were suddenly troubled and a silent question sprang into them, but her lips did not speak.

"What is it, little one?" he asked gently. "You look as if you wanted to say something."

"Oh," she said desperately, "I was wondering— But perhaps you will not like me to say it—"

"Say on, sister, I won't mind anything you say. What is it?"

Amory struggled with her own reticence and then looking bravely up again she said:

"I was wondering if—if you knew God, and the Lord Jesus? It seems such a terrible chance you are taking going off up into the clouds above strange unknown perils, unless you have Him."

The young man looked at the girl gravely, intently, all the grin gone now from his pleasant lips.

"And you think that would make a difference?" he asked seriously.

"Why, of course," she said with conviction and a wistfulness about her mouth that made him wonder.

At last he spoke gravely:

"I have never considered—God—" he said and his eyes were thoughtfully upon hers— "I have never been sure—that there was—a God!"

"But you can *know* there is!" she said as gravely. Then after an instant:

"It would be nice to know—if anything happened —that you were *His*—that you were *saved!*"

He considered this a moment thoughtfully.

"Do you think," he asked, looking deep into her face with an almost tender light in his eyes, "that if I were 'saved' as you call it, and I 'went West,' that you and I would meet again?"

"Why surely!" said Amory a sudden light like joy in her face. "But there's more than that, you know," she added wistfully, "there's God. We shall be with Him! And that will be—*wonderful!*"

This time the silence was long while the young man looked earnestly into her face. At last he spoke again:

"It seems to be well worth looking into," he said and his face had a look of purpose in it.

"Well, I must go!" he said again after a moment, and there was regret in his tone. "I'm sorry. I wish I had known you sooner. Perhaps things would have been different with me. But I'll not forget what you have said. Now, aren't you going to give me some keepsake, a sort of mascot—perhaps you would call it talisman—to take with me? How about that little book? Is it something you wouldn't like to part with?"

Amory looked down at the Testament sticking out of her trifling little blue pocket.

"No, I would *like* you to have it!" she said eagerly.

"But it's not very fresh. It's rather worn I'm afraid."

"Then I will go on wearing it," he said smiling.

She held it out to him and he enfolded her hand and the book in both of his for just an instant's warm clasp.

"But you haven't told me your name, little girl," he said, looking down into her face earnestly, "I shall need to know your name."

"It is Amory," she answered simply, like a little child, "Amory Lorrimer."

"What a beautiful name!" he said. "I like it. Goodby, Amory, until I come again. And when you think about me call me Gareth, please. It was the name my mother always called me."

Then suddenly he lifted his right hand from her clasp and stooping he reverently kissed the tips of her fingers as they lay with the book in his other hand.

"I'm wearing your book over my heart," he said smiling as he straightened up and put the little book inside his jacket. "Perhaps it will bring me good luck. I suppose you would call it 'safety.' Think of me little Amory. Will you promise?"

"I will pray for you!" she said with eyes that were shining with unbidden tears.

He gave her another quick look as if he longed to say something more, then changing his mind he suddenly sprang into the cockpit and started up his engine.

The sound of its throbbing brought Amory to her quick senses. Somebody in the house would surely hear that! She must not be seen out here thus. She suddenly backed to the hedge which was only a few feet away, and where she was at least sheltered for the moment from any curious eyes.

The great bird was running down the field away from her now, and already the stranger had become a stranger once more. She marveled as she saw it rise from the earth so confidently like a creature born to air, not earth. She could barely make out the young man's figure now, he was so far away. It made her feel so small and insignificant standing there against the hedge, her arms outspread to flatten herself as much as possible out of sight.

He was circling now and coming toward her again, rising as he came, and suddenly he was just above her leaning over smiling, and something fluttered down from his hand like a white bird. He waved and pointed to it, and circled away going up and up into the blue, and the white fluttering thing came down just above her and fluttered into her very face. Breathlessly she put up her hands and caught it, a soft silken something, and held it close, but she kept her eyes on the great bird that was throbbing away into the blue distance over the mountains.

It all seemed a dream as she looked and remembered the things he had said. Yet he *had* been talking to her, and even now her little Testament was riding up there in the sky above his heart! One hand stole down into the little empty trifling pocket. How strange it seemed! One moment here, the next moment gone! And perhaps gone so far!

"Oh, God, keep him!" she prayed softly in her heart, and thrilled to think she might keep on praying for him. There was nothing wrong in that.

So she stood breathlessly, flattened against the green wall of the hedge, watching, till the great bird became a mere speck over the mountain, and finally was lost in the light of the horizon.

Then, and not till then, did she take down the soft silken thing that she had caught to her heart as it fell, and look at it.

It was a silk handkerchief, fine and clean as if it had just been unfolded. There was something knotted in one corner. It had a blue border the color of his eyes, and its texture was delightful to touch. It spoke of wealth and luxury. And he had dropped it down for her to keep because she had given him her book. Ought she to keep it? Oh, but what else could she do? She could not take it into the house and explain where it came from and how she came to be in possession of it. But quick alarm came now to warn her. The sound of the engine might have roused the house. They might come out at any minute, and how foolish she would feel to be found there holding a man's silk handkerchief in her hands!

She stuffed it swiftly into the empty pocket, holding her hand down over it carefully. Then she started down along the hedge. There would be a way out of this field somehow without going back to the house through that garden gate.

She walked on for some distance till at last she reached a little woods on the upper edge of the flying field, which seemed to extend along back of the Whitney property, and she finally entered the grounds once more through a break in the hedge a good way above the garages.

Anxious not to meet any one, feeling almost guilty because of her recent clandestine meeting with the departed guest, she hurried breathlessly to the back entrance, and succeeded in regaining her room without actually meeting any of the family or guests, though she just escaped coming face to face with the golden haired Diana who was coming out on the terrace as she slid into the doorway of the back hall.

Up in her room she locked her door and fell on her knees beside the bed. So much seemed to have happened since she had left that room that morning, so very much. It seemed as if the whole universe was turned upside down for her. She wanted to laugh and she wanted to cry, but she wanted most of all to pray, and the words were choked in tears in her throat. All she could say was "Oh, Father, keep him safely. Save him and keep him safely."

When she grew calmer she got up from her knees and took out the handkerchief examining it more carefully. With excited fingers she unknotted the corner. Pinned safely inside was a pair of little silver wings, evidently a prize for some deed of valor. On the back was his name, Theodore Gareth Kingsley, and a date.

She looked long at it, holding it in her hand, pinning it on her dress just for a moment to see how it would seem, studying the fine engraving, wondering at herself, trembling at herself lest somehow she had done the wrong thing.

Again she arraigned herself. Nothing like this had ever come into her life before. For years Will Hazard had seen her home from prayer meeting, and Frank Burton had carried her books from school, and Sam Thomas had taken her to the Rayport High School games, and several boys had called upon her often, sometimes alone, sometimes together. But to have a stranger pick her up in this astounding way seemed all wrong. It was not according to the bringing up of Aunt Hannah and Aunt Jocelyn. She had always felt that such things would not happen to a good discreet girl. Yet this had happened to her. Was she wrong to keep these little silver wings? Ought she perhaps to fling them away in the grass, and let some other girl find them and bring them into the house some day, thinking their friend "Teddy" had lost them? But no, he had put the wings into her hand to keep. They were evidently something he cared for, as much perhaps as she cared for the little Testament that her own dear mother had given her on a birthday long ago before that mother went home to heaven. Perhaps she should not have given her Testament away, yet when he asked she had felt a heaven-sent urge to give it to him. It was God's book. It might show him the way to God.

Some girls might have given that book coquettishly, but not Amory. She was serious in all that she did, and the book meant so much to her own heart that she could not lightly give it to any one.

A clamor suddenly arose outside the window, and in new alarm Amory quickly wrapped her treasures away, the pin fastened firmly in the handkerchief, the whole wrapped in a bit of paper inside the inner pocket of her suit case. No one in this house should ever see them She would not even write to the aunts about it all for they would never understand. Perhaps, when she was back home and time had made this thing more plain, she might tell them what had happened, and get their judgment on her own actions. But no, she was not sure Aunt Hannah would understand even then. They would be grieved, the aunts, and think she had soon departed from their upbringing. They would be afraid to have her away from them a day, lest the bird-man would steal her and spirit her away.

So she locked away her treasures, and went to the window to see what the outcry was about.

It was Caroline who had started it.

"Ted isn't in his room, Mother! I knocked and knocked and then I opened the door a tiny crack and nobody was there. Christine says she heard him go down the back stairs quite early. I'll bet he has gone out to that old plane! I'll bet he's taken a fly without any of us along. And I told him it was my turn first, because he promised the last time he was here! If he has taken anybody else I'm off him for life. Is anybody missing? Where's Di? Oh, there you are! And Susanne? Well, then maybe he's gone alone, the Pig!"

She stamped her foot angrily.

Amory hovered behind her curtain guiltily and watched them all, knowing that she could so easily explain where their Teddy had gone, hugging the thought wickedly to herself that she alone of all that company had been asked to take that first flight. Glad that she had not accepted of course, but glad, glad that he had cared to ask her.

Was that wrong for her to feel glad about that? Oh, was it? She had not realized before how easy it was for her to be selfish, how romantic she could become. What on earth was the matter with her?

"Why, I'll tell you where he is of course," said Mrs. Whitney coming out smiling. "He's out on the flying field, Caroline, petting up that precious old engine of his. You ought to have looked for him there at once, for that's where he always goes the first thing in the morning."

There was an immediate stampede down through the garden to the little gate and out on the flying field. Amory standing back in her room watching them, found herself trembling, as if her recent escapade were about to be discovered; as if she herself were out there now standing with her back against that hedge, the soft kerchief in her hands, waiting to be brought to shame.

It was a relief when they all came trooping back, to realize that she was up here safe and the handkerchief hidden away from sight. They did not even know she was here, unless some one had seen her from the window when she went out very early. She had come in by such a roundabout way that surely no one would suspect her of having been with the missing guest.

She nevertheless felt guilty, as if she ought to go down and explain the absent one. It was such a relief to know she need not.

"The plane is gone, Mother! I told you so!" cried Caroline angrily. "There goes our plan for the day right at the start. There won't be even couples, and how can we play our tournament? I declare I think Ted is the limit! I didn't think he'd be mean like that. He knew what we were intending to do and he just went off without a word."

"Perhaps he'll be back," said Diana confidently. "You know he has a date with me to-night," and she threw herself down in a big picturesque chair and tilted her chin toward the sky. "He'll probably be back in time for the first game."

Then came Christine with a note.

"I found it in the library on your desk, Madam," she said.

Mrs. Whitney took it annoyedly and opened it. If he had left a note it must be he did not intend to return. It was most provoking when she had thought she had him safely for once.

Frowning she read the note aloud.

DEAR AUNT:

I'm leaving early having an imperative call to New York. If nothing interferes I'll be back in time for to-night's festivities. If not you'll know I'm hopping off to far lands and it can't be helped. In which case tell Diana Dorne I'm sorry but I couldn't help it. I didn't tell you last night because I didn't want to spoil the fun.

Apologies and affection

Ted

"Now isn't that just like him!" she said looking up vexedly. "He's quite impossible. I never could depend on him for a thing since he got this flying craze. And mercy! What is he going to do next? I nearly turned gray when he did that endurance test. I suppose we'll see it in the papers to-morrow though if he doesn't come back. Now, girls, what are we going to do to fill his place?"

"I know, Teacher," said Susanne raising her hand eagerly, "let's take the preacher and train him for the part."

"The preacher?" said Mrs. Whitney raising her eyebrows. "What preacher."

"She means John Dunleith, Mother," said Caroline with infinite scorn in her voice. "She hasn't the least idea what a nut he is!"

"Oh, John! Why, my dear Susanne. Impossible! He would run from a card as if it were a serpent and I doubt if he would know a tennis racket if he met one. Of course I haven't seen him since he was a boy and then only for a few hours, but he writes the most religious letters to your uncle, and he has had no contact with our world whatever. Of course he'll be polite and all that, I suppose; but he's a sort of recluse, I imagine, always trying to convert somebody. We really can't be burdened with trying to include him in the company. We'll have to telephone and get somebody else here quickly before he arrives, and then he will understand that our numbers are full. Of course we must be polite, but he really wouldn't do for bridge, or dancing, or even any of the sports I'm sure. Now who else is there? Tommy Hague I suppose, though he is a little too fond of cocktails, and Mr. Whitney has taken the most incredible dislike to him."

"You leave Mr. Dunleith to me, Mother Whitney!" called out Diana swinging her long slim silken leg back and forth from her lounging chair. "I'll wind him round my little finger. You don't know what I'll do to him. I might teach him to dance or I may even decide to teach him bridge, in which case nobody is to fuss if he proves terribly dumb. It's part of the game you know and we all agreed to help."

They went on planning their diabolical joke, and Amory in her room fumed indignantly and wished she knew a way to warn the young minister before he arrived and so foil their plans.

They all trooped in noisily to breakfast and she was glad to hear Christine's knock as she came in with the breakfast tray, for her early walk and exciting experiences had made her very hungry.

"Madam wishes to see you at eleven in her boudoir," she announced when she had arranged the tray on a little table for Amory. "She usually has her breakfast in bed and opens her mail before she gets up. She will want you then to take dictation. But this morning she took a notion to get up to breakfast so she can't see you till eleven. She said I was to tell you that you were to feel free to go to the library and get anything you want to read."

Amory thanked her pleasantly and sat down to her breakfast with a good appetite in spite of the turmoil of her mind.

CHAPTER IV

WHEN she was through she looked at her watch. It was half past nine, and there would just be time before she was summoned to Mrs. Whitney to write a letter home to the dear aunts who would be watching and waiting hourly for the first word from her. Could she do it without showing so much as a hint of the excitement of the morning? Would she be able to keep all that incident of the flier out of the very atmosphere of her letter? Well, she must try, though she suspected that Aunt Jocelyn would find out. Aunt Jocelyn during the years had always somehow managed to find out everything in her life. It was hard to deceive a love so understanding and true.

But this was something that must be kept from her at least while she was away, for it would only plant a seed of uneasiness that would give infinite pain to the two dear women, pain for which there was no need, and uneasiness which had absolutely no foundation. For of course she would never see that flier again, and of course she must treat the incident as a mere opportunity to send forth her little Testament to plant a possible seed in a heart that needed it.

So she wrote her letter, full of lovely descriptions, mountains and castles, and mansions. Oh, such mansions, and the country club! The flying field figured only as a bit of the landscape next door with the wonder of a plane landing in full view. That was as much as she permitted herself to put in. If ever the rest of the story came to light it would be easier to have mentioned that landing plane as a simple incident and nothing that had to be hid.

The letter was further filled with character sketches of the guests of the house as she saw them on the terrace from her window, and closed with a detailed description of her room. On the whole she felt that she had done pretty well, and was just addressing her envelope when the sound of an automobile arriving at the porte cochere, just beyond the terrace and visible from her window, sent her to her curtained point of observation again. And it was so she saw the arrival of the much discussed and unwelcome cousin.

There was nothing awkward or gawky about the

stranger's appearance. Perhaps this was not he after all. Perhaps it was a substitute for Teddy whom they had raked up from somewhere by telephone. Only this was the hour when they had said he would arrive. What was the pleasant sounding name by which they called him? Dunleith, that was it, John Dunleith! It had a Scotch sound and smacked of heather and noble Norman blood or something like that. She felt hazy in her knowledge of things Scotch. But she liked his face, as much as she saw of it, as he got out of the car and went up the steps. He had a square firm chin, and pleasant lips, not rippling into a grin like the flier's, but graver, more settled perhaps. Nice gray eyes too, and a clear cut face. He was tall, and did not have the ascetic look she had expected from his relatives' description.

He wore a plain gray business suit, tweed of a good cut, and there was nothing in the least countrified about him, neither did he have the pale fine frenzied look of a fanatic. In fact he appeared like a real man with good sound common sense, so far as a first casual glance went. But probably she was wrong and it wasn't John Dunleith at all.

A few minutes later she was summoned into Mrs. Whitney's boudoir, and there sat the man she had just seen arrive.

Mrs. Whitney received her graciously, coolly, and introduced her quite casually to the man:

"My nephew Mr. Dunleith, Miss Lorrimer. I am going to ask you later to show him around the place, as I shall be busy myself, and I believe the other young people are all busy elsewhere. You can ask Christine to direct you, in case you haven't already discovered your way around."

Then she turned to the young man.

"John, if you have letters to write suppose you go to your room and get them done now. Michael goes down to the office about noon and can take them for you, and Miss Lorrimer and I will get through the morning mail while you are writing. I'll have some one call you when Miss Lorrimer is at leisure."

And so, that was the way the lady was going to get around her unwelcome nephew, put him off on her secretary! She found herself inwardly rebelling, not that she did not like the appearance of the young man, but it had not occurred to her that her social life would be ordered for her in this way. However, it might be a good thing, for perhaps she might be able to save the young man from the practical joke that was awaiting him. Still, he did not look like a young man who needed protection, and perhaps her sympathy was all unnecessary.

She sat down at the desk that Mrs. Whitney indicated and prepared to get to work on the pile of mail that lay in a mahogany tray, trying to forget all young men and attend strictly to business. After all she must remember that she was here on a salary, a good salary too, and that whatever she did, even to entertain a young man, it was purely business and nothing personal in it at all, not even if he were an aviator, she added severely.

Mrs. Whitney spoke pleasantly of Amory's recommendations, and said she hoped they would get along well together. She then went on to business crisply with a keen logical mind that grasped any situation immediately, and knew what she wanted to do about it.

Amory jotted down notes on the envelopes of the letters, one after another. There was nothing important. They were mostly society notes, and some bills to be attended to. There was a pile of cards to be sent out for a tea next week, and a long list of addresses; a package to be returned to a city shop with instructions about its exchange; a note of complaint to a dressmaker; and an order for several pairs of shoes. It wasn't difficult work, and the whole session took not more than half an hour.

"And now Miss Lorrimer," said her employer, "I hope you'll make yourself quite at home. You will take your meals usually in the little breakfast room, though I may call upon you sometimes to fill in a place at dinner when a guest is lacking you know. I suppose you have evening dresses, and if you haven't the right thing just ask Christine and she will get you something. The girls and I have loads of things we don't wear any more, and Christine is quite clever with her needle. Don't hesitate to use her whenever you need her. You'll find her quite willing and she understands what is needed. You play bridge well I suppose? We may need you to take a hand now and then to fill in."

Amory's color stole softly up as she answered: "No, Mrs. Whitney, I don't play."

"You don't? How odd! But it's of no consequence. We probably won't need you. Don't you dance either? Well, perhaps that's just as well. My nephew naturally doesn't either, being a preacher of course, though there are some ministers nowadays who are quite broad-minded about such simple amusements. But it will be as well to have some one for John to talk to when the other young people are busy. You play tennis do you, or golf?"

"Tennis, oh yes," said Amory with a relieved smile, "and golf a little too, though I've never had much time to practice that."

"Well, they may want you for a set sometime you know. And I believe your recommendations said you had a nice voice and played a little? Music is always helpful, and not every one wants to oblige of course, so you may be useful that way. I don't mind telling you I like your appearance, and you seem to have a pleasant way with you. Of course you're—rather too good-looking for a secretary but I guess you will be discreet and not let that get in your way, my dear. And now run along and take my nephew around for a little while before you get at the letters, for I don't want him to feel neglected. I'll leave it to you to see that he doesn't get lonely, the young people are always so careless. I've had a typewriter sent to your room for the business letters, and if you need anything for your work just ask Christine. That's all I believe, and I think we're going to get along finely together."

Amory found herself in the hall with a great sheaf of letters and a feeling of heavy responsibility resting upon her. So it seemed she was to be a social goat as well as secretary. Well, she would do her best, for there was the wonderful salary, and the dear aunts needing it so much, and she mustn't fail for a mere matter of being a lady, but where in the world was she to find the young man whom she was to escort over the place, and how could she show off a place she did not know herself?

She was about to seek Christine for information when the young man himself came down the hall.

He smiled and she liked him even better than when she had first seen him.

"You were detailed, I believe, to show me around," he said pleasantly, "but if you'll excuse me, I've got a lot of work I'd like to do, and you look as if you had quite a handful yourself. Suppose we call this off and both of us do our work."

She smiled up at him understandingly.

"All right," she said, "that suits me wonderfully. This is my first day here, and I'm not so accustomed to things yet as to be sure I'll get everything done on time. Besides, it would be like the blind leading the blind for me to take you around this place for I don't know it yet myself."

"Well, then, perhaps we can reverse the orders some time when we are not so busy, and I can show you around. My aunt forgets that I was here once for a whole summer when I was a kid and she was in Europe, and I'll wager I know some parts of the place better than she does."

So they parted pleasantly and Amory went to her room. wondering if after all she ought not to have taken that opportunity to somehow warn the young man of what was to come. Only how could she have said it? And surely, surely they would not dare to play such a prank on one who seemed so much of a man. They could not make a fool out of him. He had too much common sense. She was going to like him, she felt sure. He was just friendly and nice, and she could feel at home with him. There was nothing of the romance of the flier man about him, but he was strong and true and wholesome. One could see that at a glance. Yes, and a gentleman too, every inch of him. And she need not worry about that silly plan for making a fool of him. As soon as they saw him they would understand that he was no country gawk, and of course would abandon their silly joke.

She settled down to her work at the desk near the window.

The typewriter had come and was a good one, new and one of the best makes. It delighted her to work with it. The one she had at home was a second hand affair that she had bought for ten dollars and was sadly in need of repair. It was a joy to work with good implements, and she turned off the business part of her mail rapidly.

She had done about half of the other correspondence when voices chimed out in a chorus as several of the guests came across the lawn from the direction of the tennis courts. As they trooped up on the terrace a boy about twelve years old came out of the door and called out to his sister. Amory had seen him once or twice before and had surmised he must be the youngest Whitney child.

"Hey! Car'lin, bet you don't know who's come!"

The voice conveyed an unmistakable delight in the arrival.

"Who?" called back the sister suddenly arrested in a laughing combat with one of the young men. "Who, Neddy? Tell me quick! Did Mother succeed in getting Barry Blaine? She was telephoning when we left."

"Aw, naw. Gosh no! Not him. It's cousin John! He just came, and he's going fishing with me this afternoon. You needn't think you're going to get him."

"Great Cats! Has he come already? Mother didn't expect him till night. Now the goose is cooked! Dad is coming home and he'll insist on our trotting him round everywhere with us!" said Caroline in a disgusted tone.

"Oh, has he come?" said Diana vivaciously. "That's good! Don't worry about little Johnny, darling. I'll take him off your hands. I'll go fishing too. That will be all that could be desired in the way of a beginning. Lucky I played off my set this morning. Let me see, what does one wear fishing to be fetching? Green?"

"My eye! You won't go fishing with us!" growled Ned suddenly roused to understand the situation. "We don't want *gurrls!* Scarin' the fish! And fallin' in the water! You can just lay off this expedition. I'm tellin' ya!"

"Oh, that's all right, Neddy," patronized Diana gleefully, "you just run off and tell your mother you want a stick of candy. I'm running this fishing trip. See?"

Ned glared. His face was fairly purple with rage, and his eyes were stormy.

"Well, I guess you'll find out!" he bleated, and turning on his rubber heel fled to find his cousin John.

"Tra-la-la!" trilled Diana. "I'm going up to dress for fishing, girls. Behold me when I return but don't exclaim. Remember, the game's on. All set?"

And Diana disappeared into the house.

The other girls followed her, and presently the silver gong for lunch sounded, and Christine came to call Amory to the breakfast room to eat her own solitary lunch.

As she sat down to the apple green table in a charming bay-window looking out on the garden, and began to eat a cunningly devised salad with little delectable hot biscuits, she saw two figures steal out of the door that led from the back stairs and hurry across the garden, out the gate, and down the flying field toward the woods. One was the boy Ned, bare of foot, triumphant of visage, wearing a khaki suit apparently hastily donned, and bearing a tin can and a fishing rod. The other was the tall, newly arrived cousin John Dunleith, in a flannel shirt and khaki trousers, also bearing fishing rods and tackle.

As they disappeared toward the woods Amory smiled amusedly. Score one for the preacher! Diana would have to change her costume this time for she was not getting asked on this fishing trip. Ned apparently "knew his onions" as the saying went, and had not waited on the order of lunch. Perhaps she had failed to notice a large cracker box carried carefully under young Ned's arm, containing hastily foraged sustenance, mostly cake. But she knew from the very set of both of their backs that to the two who were going fishing, lunch played a very minor part in the doings of this present day.

A moment later the waitress went hastily through the breakfast room and swung the door excitedly into the butler's pantry.

"Where's Christine?" she called, "Madam wants her to go right up to Mr. Dunleith's room and call him. He hasn't come down to lunch yet and they're sitting down. She's to call Mr. Neddy too, and see that his hands and face are washed. Are the biscuits ready to go in?" and she returned as hastily bearing a linen covered dish.

It was like watching a drama unfold, Amory thought, as she ate her delicious meal and looked dreamily out the window toward the woods where the two figures had safely vanished from sight. Well, the Diana girl was foiled for another half day at least and though she didn't in the least care of course about any of them, still she couldn't help being a little glad that the man had escaped. For she thought she could judge from his face that he would hate to have that girl along—that is if he really loved fishing.

But Amory did not know Diana if she thought she was foiled. Diana never gave up when she had once decided on a certain course, and she generally won whatever goal she had set.

Amory had gone back to her desk with a zeal to finish the first day's stint on time, and was working hard addressing envelopes from her list when the young people streamed out to the terrace after their leisurely lunch.

Diana in slim Lincoln green, of soft clinging silk, dress and stockings to match, with little suede oxfords of exactly the same shade of green, stretched lazily in the long willow lounging chair, and let the afternoon sunshine lay bright hands on her gold hair, while she looked off thoughtfully through half closed fringes to the distant mountains. When she chose to open those fringes for a moment and gaze at some one, her eyes seemed to have taken on a subtle change. They were by no means as indifferent as her attitude would lead one to suppose, and they had caught a hint of jade from her costume.

Amory watched her half admiringly. She was really lovely. The soft pink in her cheeks was put on so delicately that it might even have been there by nature, and her lips were only accentuated in one tiny point to show their pouting loveliness. She wore no jewelry of any kind, not even a ring. She certainly had dressed perfectly for the part of a fisher-lady de luxe. It was a pity that she could not have had the audience she had evidently craved. Yet much as she was forced to admire her charm, Amory could not forgive her for having fallen so easily into the star part of the plot formed against a stranger. It was utterly against all the codes in which Amory had been trained, and it seemed despicable to her. Therefore she could not but rejoice that this first attempt had failed.

The young people lingered idly, smoking and chattering, and openly killing time till the hour should arrive for the next tennis set at the country club.

At last one of the young men spoke, eyeing Diana restlessly.

"Better call off this deal, Diana," he said carelessly. "The game isn't worth the candle anyway. Come on down to the country club and do eighteen holes with me. I'm in fine shape now and I want to show off my strokes."

"Are you getting cold feet, Freddie?" said Diana looking at him insolently from between gold fringes, a jade sparkle in her eyes.

"Cold feet? Why, no, what have I got to do with it except be bored? What's a Dunleith or two in my young life? I say call it off. This fellow is evidently fully able to entertain himself and our obligation is quite fulfilled I'd say. Don't hang around here for something that isn't going to come. If this precious cousin has gone fishing he won't return till dark, my word for it, and you know that's true."

"Oh, did you think I was waiting around for him?" asked Diana sweetly. "You're much mistaken. I'm staying to rest and do a few things of my own."

"Well, it's no good waiting for Ted either," complained Fred daringly, despite the dangerous green in Diana's eyes. "If Ted comes back we can hear his plane as well at the country club as here, and I'll give you my word I'll get you back at once if he comes. Come on and have some golf."

"Since when did you think yourself constituted to be my guardian, Freddie dear?" asked Diana lazily. "I wouldn't advise you to try to keep it up. You'd find it is a fairly large proposition."

"I should say!" murmured a disgruntled youth rising and flinging away his cigarette. He spoke as out of a large experience, and walked away where he could lean against an ivied wall by an arched gateway, and watch the lady from afar. They had all been worshipers at Diana's feet. Amory could readily see that.

Presently the group dragged themselves from their comfortable positions and walked off by twos and threes to the country club to see the afternoon doubles played. But Diana remained in her chair, a slim green graceful figure, apparently enjoying utter relaxation.

"You won't change your mind and come, Di," called Susanne from down by the dahlia gardens.

"No thanks, Sue darling, not this afternoon!" said Diana and drowsed off again.

When they were all out of hearing she opened her eyes cautiously and looked around, then stealthily slipped into the house. Five minutes later she appeared below again, a neat little knapsack of wicker wear strapped from her shoulder, a trig and up to date fishing rod in her hand, a soft slouch hat of Lincoln green over her bright head, and a determined look on her rose tipped lips.

She walked briskly and silently down the garden to the flying field, and turned her steps quite resolutely toward the woods as if she knew exactly where she was going. Quite as if she might have watched two figures go that way a little over an hour before.

Amory watched her from her window, resting her hand a moment from her writing. Such a trim, slender, boylike figure, with determined back, and graceful gait like a young Robin Hood. She could not but admire her, and she wondered with a smile of amusement on her lips, what would happen when the green fisheress appeared in the wood, supposing she were successful in her quest? How would the man with the strong chin take this interruption? What could he possibly do about it anyway if she was there?

The summer day settled drowsily, dreamily into afternoon. There were bees below in the garden dipping into honeysuckle and roses. Their droning made a pleasant accompaniment to a meadow lark far off. Sweet perfumes wafted up from the garden, and the shimmer of light and color and warm sunshine sifted in at her open window and made Amory hungry for some of the life and joy and pleasant things that the other young people were having. She rebuked herself and plodded away at the pile of envelopes that had to be addressed, for it had been impressed upon her that they must be finished promptly.

But now and again her eyes would stray to the distant mountains, and rest on the great space of clear blue sky into which the flier had disappeared that morning.

How far away that morning seemed now, and how unreal! Perhaps after all she had only dreamed it. Perhaps there was no silk handkerchief guarding a pair of little silver wings hid away in her suit case guiltily. Perhaps it was all a vision of the night.

At last so strong was the drawing that she laid down her pen, made sure her door was locked and went and took out the wings again, holding them softly in the palm of her hand, reading the name inscribed on the back, Theodore Gareth Kingsley. Gareth. A beautiful name. And he had asked her to use it when she thought of him. The others called him Teddy. Gareth. Why, that was the name of one of King Arthur's knights, the one with the great determination, wasn't it? She must read up about it again. Doubtless his mother had some hidden meaning when she liked to call him that, unless indeed it was a family name. She would browse around down in that great library by and by and see if there was a copy of Knights of King Arthur and the Round Table, and read up. It would be something pleasant to do when she finished her work. She must keep busy here or she would be deadly lonely.

As she sat holding the little silver wings in her hand she thought of her Testament, gone forth from her. Would it do any work for the kingdom anywhere? Would the young man read it at all? He had asked for it more in the way of sentimentality. He did not even seem to know what it was. He had called it a "little book." It would have meant just as much to him if it had been a volume of essays or Shakespeare. Would he ever open it? Or would he wear it superstitiously as a protection from danger, the way ignorant people wore a rabbit's foot on a ribbon around their necks?

Suddenly she laid the silver trinket down upon her bed, and dropped on her knees beside it. She had promised to pray for him, and her heart at that moment went out with a great longing that he might know God, and understand what it meant to be a saved one; that he might be protected and guarded from the dangers of the air, the perils of the sea, and brought back safely; or if not, then saved and brought Home.

She was surprised at herself for the fervor of her petition. She had often prayed earnestly for the conversion of friends, of her Sunday School class, but had never felt such a strong impulse to beg for God's mercy on any other as she now felt. It was as if she suddenly realized his great need; as if the perils of his profession—or was it only his play? She did not know—had taken a deep hold upon her, and something outside herself was urging her to prayer, urging her to a new faith, that filled her with a kind of exaltation, that even brought tears to her eyes as she prayed. She did not understand herself. She was half ashamed of herself to pray so earnestly for one who was an utter stranger to herself. Was she falling for the things he had said that morning? Was she losing her head to a pair of handsome eyes, and a strong chin? To pleasant words and a taking way? Was she just like other fool girls after all? Had it done her no good to be brought up by dear Aunts Hannah and Jocelyn? "Oh, God, forgive me if I am a fool!" she prayed. "And I know I must be for I never acted this way before, but please take care of Gareth, and save him for Thyself."

She got up from her knees then and firmly put away the wings as if they were something she ought not to look upon. She even locked her suit case, and then went soberly back to her work, and applied herself so assiduously, that only now and then did her eyes stray to the far blue spaces out her window, where she had seen the great bird disappear that morning. It was presumable that if he should return he would come back the same way, and he ought to be arriving within the next hour or two. If he should come, how must she conduct herself? How was she to keep out of his way? For that their acquaintance should go no further was of course the only possible thing under the circumstances. She must get away from the thought of him. And if he returned she must give back those wings of course.

Or should she? It might look as if she wanted her Testament back again, and if it could do him any possible good she wanted him to keep it. Perhaps it would be better just to keep out of sight and ignore the whole thing if he returned.

Nevertheless her eyes would stray now and then to the far-away blue, but no dim speck in the distance drew near and developed into a great ship as on the day before, and the shadows grew long on the grass, the young people returned from the country club, and still the bird-man had not come.

CHAPTER V

Down in the woods near the ravine Miss Robin Hood stumbled along on her little high heeled Lincoln green suede shoes and set her lips more firmly. She knew these shoes were not designed for climbing down ravines nor for fishing along a muddy stream, but she had bigger fish to catch than mere brook trout, and the shoes were a part of her outfit, so she bore the discomfort, and set her lips.

It was somewhat of a puzzle to know which way to turn, but Diana was a girl of unerring instincts and she followed those now and they brought her out at last, down stream, to a quiet pool that looked deep and cool and only flecked with dimpling sunshine here and there; a pool where hemlocks dipped and touched their dripping fronds, where great rocks wore velvet moss and gray lichens, and where great trees canopied and arched above, harboring a silver toned thrush or two to send a wild sweet note upward now and then even when there was no ear but God's to hear.

She walked quietly, for she wished to come on her quarry unaware, and stealing through the cool shadows of the wooded hillside in her Lincoln green, she seemed like a part of the landscape. No one would have noticed her, not even a bird or a chipmunk would have fled from her, because she looked like one of them, and quite as if she might have been cousin to a tree. So going, she came at last to where she sighted them, sitting silently together on a rock, the young man and the boy, their lines dropped, their faces intent, the filtering sunbeams touching their heads with flecks of light and bringing out their statue-like attitudes.

She dropped down silently behind a group of cedars where she was not visible and watched them intently a while. As motionless as the fishers she sat and studied the man to whom she meant to lay siege.

It surprised her that he was so well built, and that his head was so finely shaped. She somehow had expected him to be of the ascetic type, and awkward. His aunt had intimated that he had had few advantages and she had supposed of course this would show in his general attitude.

But this man was no hobbledehoy.

Of course, if he had been brought up in the country—she was not just sure Mrs. Whitney had said he had—he would naturally be more at his ease in overalls on the brink of a stream fishing, than in evening clothes in a salon. But this man had an innate grace about him that held her admiration, and when he suddenly jerked up his line and landed a great fish on the bank beside him, to the exquisite joy of his young companion his hearty laugh rang out with a cultured note that surprised her. But of course, a preacher! He must have studied somewhere and been with cultured people at least for a time. She ought to have thought of that. Well, that only made her task the easier.

For a long time she sat and watched him, noting his kindly way with the boy, noting the admiration in Neddy's eyes, and the hearty way the man accepted him as a pal, without the least condescension or impatience. Then she slowly, stealthily, arose and began her soft descent to the bank opposite the two on the rock. She noted carefully the lay of the land. The stream narrowed just across from the rock where the man and the boy sat. There were clumps of laurel and hemlock clustering thick on her side of the stream.

She descended carefully, a step or two at a time, taking pains not to step on a dry twig, or a loose stone, and she kept persistently behind trees and bushes, and so descending she finally reached their level, behind the foliage, and parting almost imperceptibly the branches, was able at last to wedge herself in between the hemlocks and get her head and shoulders into full view without having disturbed the two intent fishers. A chameleon could have done no better.

So there she stood before them in her perfect setting, Lincoln green against Lincoln green, a vivid little face under the Robin Hood soft hat, with the jade lights in her eyes, and the flecks of sunlight caught in her eyelashes. She could not have made it all more perfect if she had hired the scenery painted for this her first act in the farce she was to play. Or was it to be tragedy? She had scarcely planned so far. And so she stood and waited for the right moment and the curtain to rise.

The curtain rose when Ned landed his first fish, swinging his line in a great circle, and bellowing his voice out so loud it frightened the thrushes far above. Two laughs rang out, a young joyous one, and an older happy one, blending as if they enjoyed each other and loved the day. Two laughs like music, that suddenly stopped with a crash in the middle and brought a silence that almost hurt.

While it hurt and held, a thrush high up gave a fluted far-away note, and the wind swept soft fingers over a lute in the trees, and the man and the boy looked at the fisher-lady standing between the parted branches of the hemlocks, with her little brown grass creel strapped across her shoulders, and her soft green hat pushed back showing the gold of her hair, like the fringes of her jade green eyes, and her trig little rod in her hands. Nothing could have been more startling to a silent fisherman and boy than to find a wood nymph caught thus in the branches watching them when they thought they were quite alone with the distant thrushes.

"Great Cats!" ejaculated the boy when he had rubbed his eyes and found that she was real. "Isn't this the limit!"

"Go softly, old Pard!" said the low voice of the man. "We must remember that we are men, gentlemen you know. Cut this kid stuff!"

The girl across the stream did not fail to get this, every word, and to be astonished at it. Neither did she fail to notice the firm chin and pleasant mouth, the keen gray eyes, and the fine white teeth that flashed as the man smiled. This was going to be interesting, far beyond her highest hopes.

But she did not leave the situation too long without explanation. She knew the exact instant when the action should begin.

"I didn't mean to disturb you," she said, and her voice was like a silver ribbon unrolling. "I was trying to find a good place to fish, and I came on you suddenly, so I waited till you got a bite. I'll just go on down stream now."

"You can't find a better spot than just below where you're standing," said the man, and she noted the culture of his voice. "There's a rock over there will make quite a good seat, and the fish are biting nicely right here. No reason why you shouldn't share our luck," he added heartily.

"Oh Heck!" said Neddy casting a baleful glance across the stream.

"Steady, old Pard!" advised the elder voice in an undertone.

Diana parted the branches and came forth, green clinging silken garments, slim green legs, little woodsy green shoes, and stood timorously on the rock, her green hat crowded back, her gold hair glinting with the sunbeams, and the green and gold lights in her eyes. She knew she was a picture. She was depending a good deal on that first impression, and she saw he got it. Then she dropped down prettily on the rock and was satisfied.

"Have you bait?" he asked affably.

"I had a worm," she said sweetly, "but I'm not sure but it may have got away. My creel fell off once, up on the hill."

She was fumbling with the fastener of her basket. The young man did not smile.

"Here, Kid, get this can across to her. You're barefoot!" he said as if she were another boy and quite welcome to be of their party.

Neddy sulkily took the rusty can and stepped across the wet stones above the stream, handing out grudgingly a handful of squirming angle worms in a gingerly paw, with a look of disgust on his disappointed countenance.

Diana bravely selected a squirming worm with the tips of her fingers, and endeavored nonchalantly to apply it to a fierce looking hook she had extracted from her creel.

"Bait the lady's hook for her, Pard," ordered the man dropping a silent line into the cool dark depths again.

Neddy skillfully adjusted the worm with his grubby fingers and made good his exit from that side of the stream, slithered up beside the man, and turned his back sharply toward the girl.

Diana tried to drop her line into the water,

silently, nonchalantly, as the man had done, and a deep quiet settled down upon the trio.

Little queer flies with gauzy wings skated over the surface of the water like phantoms, soft spots of light played hide and seek across the pool, and the silver throated thrushes began to spill their music from the tree top again. The girl sat and waited, and something of the quiet miracle of the woods stole into her fleshly little soul and brought a wonder.

She looked across at the silent man, his strong face bent steadily to the stream, as if that were the only thing in the universe that were of any moment now. She looked through the fringes of her golden lashes, with the hidden jade light in her eyes, but she seemed to be looking deep into the stream, just as the man and the boy were doing, and waiting.

A long time they sat so, while the thrushes spilled their music down the silences, and the tall tree played its lute, and then a dimple dotted the water, and the man's line swung up another gallant fish.

The boy did not whoop this time. He only grunted sulkily, mannishly, as if it were a matter of little moment, a matter to be quite expected and not to be rejoiced about, but there was a set of satisfaction about his young shoulders, and the round cheek and chin, that showed as he sat twisted away from the intruder.

No period in her life that Diana could remember had ever impressed or thrilled her as did that quiet cool afternoon she spent in utter silence, with a good looking strange young man and an angry boy across the stream from her, neither of whom looked at her nor spoke for whole half hours together. She had not thought that any young man could be indifferent like that.

But she was game. She sat her rock in silence,

and held her borrowed rod with a hand that ached from unaccustomedness, and caught nothing at all. Moment by moment, hour after hour passed, and the shadows grew deep in the woods. Were they never going home? She did not mean to go till they did. The crowd would be home from the country club by now. They would be wondering where she was. She could tell by the little wrist watch that was partly visible under her green sleeve, that it was time to dress for dinner, but she held her ground. She meant to arrive at the house attended by the hero, in full view of an admiring multitude, even if she had to make a hurried toilet later for the evening.

At last the man spoke.

"Haven't we some grub, Kid? I'm getting hungry, aren't you?"

The boy produced a grubby cracker box and opened it.

"We'll have to divide with the lady you know, Pard," said the pleasant voice of the man.

"Oh Heck!" said the boy with a more than audible sigh, "I 'spose so if you say so," and he eyed the cake longingly.

"I have a box of chocolates," said the lady sweetly.

"That might help," said the man, "how about it, Pard?"

"I druther have cake," said Ned grumpily.

"But I'd rather have chocolates, so suppose you have my share of cake, and I have your share of chocolates? How about it?"

Ned's smile came muddily out, and he looked adoringly into the man's face. The girl watching with the jade gold lights in her eyes, felt a sudden pang of jealousy for the bond between these two whose afternoon she was distinctly conscious she had spoiled. It hurt her pride terribly to acknowledge it to herself, but she knew that they would *both* rather have been left alone. She had never met with quite such a slap in the face before. Men usually wanted her on all occasions.

They divided the cake and the chocolates amicably, and sat pleasantly munching.

"I thought fairies had come true again," said the man suddenly with a rare smile. "You looked just like a wood nymph out of a fairy tale."

She looked up astonished, almost embarrassed. The men she knew did not talk of fairy tales. They never had read any. What kind of a man was this, in this nineteenth century modern world, talking of fairies and nymphs?

"But now," said the man, when the last chocolate and crumb of cake was finished, "see, Kid, the lady has caught no fish. We must get the lady a catch before we go home. This isn't polite at all for us men to catch all the fish."

Ned put his tongue in his cheek and eyed his idol reflectively.

"Hand me that can of bait, son," he went on, leaning over and pulling up his own line.

Carefully he arranged the bait on his own hook, swung himself across the stepping stones and placed the rod in the lady's hand, taking her own rod from her and laying it aside.

"There!" said he, "try this. Drop it so, down there!"

Ned, face downward on the opposite rock, watched superciliously, proud of his partner, yet jealous that a moment should be wasted on a fool girl.

And sure enough a fish did bite, and in great excitement was landed on the rock, a splendid fat little bass with glistening pinkish-gold sides. Diana was filled with awe, and half afraid of the slippery scaly creature, for to tell the truth she had never gone fishing before. She had filched the rod and the creel from the house, and sacrificed a Paris creation for the occasion, and now she was afraid of her fish!

On the whole Diana was more than subdued as she walked meekly back with the two men fishers, carrying her own fish gingerly from the string they had put him on.

The sun was down when they came out into the flying field, and the twilight beginning to fall. Lights were streaming out from the great house as they entered the garden gate, and the girls in dance frocks were gathering out on the terrace.

"Here she comes!" announced Caroline loudly, "Girls! See what's here! She's got him! She went fishing after all. Leave it to Diana. Oh, but she's tho sly bird!"

"Fish!" yelled Doris. "She's really caught a fish! Or else she bribed somebody to let her carry it."

John Dunleith stood back in his brown flannel shirt and his khaki trousers, with his string of fish, and his nice gray eyes on them all.

"Tell 'em she caught it herself, Pard," he murmured in Neddy's ear, and Neddy obediently swaggered forward:

"Naw, yer all wrong this time. She caught it herself all righty," he explained, doing the honors in his best style and then added:

"Say, I guess you all don't know my cousin John yet, do ya? Meet the gang, Pard!" and he swept a comprehensive gesture about the group.

It was not till then that Mrs. Whitney hurried out and made apologies.

"Oh, is that you John? I suppose you've met all these young people, haven't you? We have searched the house to find you. I suppose Neddy carried you off. I hope you haven't been too bored. Oh, Diana, you don't mean you went fishing too? How kind of you. But you were so tired—"

A warning look from Caroline stopped her mother's tongue for the instant and Diana broke in in the nick of time:

"Oh, I've had a most glorious time, Mother Whitney. I never knew it was so restful to fish, and to think I've brought you home a fish! Will you have it cooked for breakfast?"

"Of course child. And now run in quick and change. Dinner is served at once. Hurry please won't you, John?"

And this was all the introduction this gray eyed nephew of the house received. Amory watching from her window of vantage was indignant for him. But a moment later there came a message from Mrs. Whitney. Her presence was required at the table for dinner, as Mr. Theodore had not yet returned, and the table was already set and could not be changed without much trouble.

So Amory flew into her white chiffon, pinned a pink silk rose on her shoulder, fastened her little string of pearls about her throat, and stepped into her white slippers as she smoothed her hair. She arrived rather breathlessly and a bit scared, in the big reception hall just as they all were going out to dinner.

The hostess made scant ceremony of the introductions. "My new secretary, Miss Lorrimer, girls," and most of the young people merely nodded and went on talking, but it was a relief to know that it was over, and she was occupying a normal position before the guests.

She found to her surprise that she was seated beside John Dunleith, and that Diana was far at the other end beside their host whom Amory now saw for the first time.

It was rather overpowering, that first dinner, for Amory was not accustomed to large affairs, and to manage all those spoons and forks, and not do anything queer, was job enough for any secretary fresh from a sweet plain home, in a little country village.

But it was to John Dunleith that she owed her peace of mind during that dinner. He simply would not let her shrink into herself as she began to do the moment she sat down. He acted like a friend and brother. He kept up a pleasant vein of friendly talk; asked her questions about the different people at the table; and when he found that she was as ignorant as he, made that a bond of friendliness between them and began to chat of affairs in the world in which every one was interested, and then of books.

She perceived that he had a vein of humor running through everything he said, and so the dinner went on and she lost her self consciousness and began really to enjoy herself.

Then, looking up, she caught the wide glance of Diana Dorne's blue eyes upon her. For they were sea blue to-night, like the exquisite frock she was wearing, a mist of blue malines which set off her lovely white shoulders like the setting of a jewel. Wide eyed innocence was the part she was playing to-night, though her cheeks were rouged and her lips were redder than nature had made them, but the jewels she wore were simple and flashed decorously, making her by far the most distinguished girl at the table.

Amory wondered that her companion did not seem to notice her at all, but he was giving all his attention to herself, and really it was pleasant.

Of course it was interesting to be down among

them all hearing what they said, and taking part in the gay scene, yet she was not really a part, and Amory wished in her heart that she was out of it. She could enjoy a talk with this gray eyed man at her side, and she could enjoy her morning's meeting with the young flier on his field, but all those girls ignoring her so sweetly did cut, in spite of her very best philosophy. Why was it that girls always did things like that? It would be so much pleasanter if she did not have to sit here and eat with them all, knowing that they all knew she was merely here to fill up an empty seat. Or was that all? Had Mrs. Whitney some quiet idea of keeping her nephew from Diana Dorne's clutches, and of using her for the purpose of keeping the two apart? Diana looked as if she might suspect that, also, for as often as Amory looked up she saw the girl in blue watching her.

And now the talk turned upon the aviator. It was Mr. Whitney who asked about him.

"Why, I thought Ted was to be here!" he said as he looked down the length of the table.

"He was," said Caroline sorely, "but he flew!"

"Flew?" said Mr. Whitney. "Not another record hop, I hope?"

"Who knows?" said his wife laughing. "He left one of his characteristic enigmatical notes. It is on my desk in the library. You can study it out at your leisure. Doubtless the morning paper will inform us soon if you can't unravel the mystery. But he may come in any minute now, you know. He promised to be back for dinner if he could. I believe he has a date with Diana here for the evening, so there is still hope."

"Oh, yes," replied Diana, "he'll be back. He is down for the first dance with me. He ought to be here any minute now!" and she shot a glance down the table at the fisherman-preacher, but John Dunleith did not lift so much as an eyelash in her direction. He went on quoting poetry to Amory, and some of it was convulsing. It hit off so well some of the things the people at the table were saying, and the way they looked and acted. Amory could hardly keep from choking in her wild desire to laugh out at him. He certainly was rare company, and could say the keenest things without cracking a smile, sometimes scarcely moving his lips. How utterly surprised the whole table would be if they could only hear him! It really was most interesting to listen to him.

But Amory's mind was not wholly on what he was saying, nor yet on the gay scene about her. She was thinking of two little silver wings hidden away in her suit case upstairs, and of the young aviator who had sailed away so gayly that morning and left them with her.

Where was he now, with his boyish grin and his blue eyes? Was he sailing the skies on his way back, or preparing to enter into unknown perils over uncharted tracks?

And what would all those people at the table say if they knew about the little silver wings that she had safely hidden away? She could not get away from the consciousness that she had them, and that he had her Testament, her little old Testament that she had had since childhood. It was a queer exchange, and she could scarcely believe that it had ever happened, although it was not yet much more than twelve hours away.

The talk drifted back to the flier once more as they rose from the table at last.

"Let's go out and see if we can sight him," proposed Caroline. "I thought I heard a plane just now. He usually gets back from New York about this time or sooner."

They drifted outside into the moonlit night, and suddenly Amory who had drifted along with the rest, with John Dunleith just behind her, saw that Diana Dorne had somehow got between them and was smiling up into the man's face.

"I haven't thanked you yet," she said prettily.

John Dunleith looked down pleasantly, as he might have looked at a little child who had spoken to him.

"Thanked me?" he said pleasantly, "for what?"

"Why, for helping me with that fish. I should have been terribly disappointed not to have caught a thing."

"Oh, *that!*" he said, "that was nothing!" but Amory thought she saw a kind of puzzled curiosity in his eyes as he studied the other girl, yet admiration too, but with it a holding aloof. Did he read her shallowness, and trickery, or ought she to give him some kind of a warning? Yet why should she? It was no concern of hers, and likely he wouldn't believe her if she should tell him the whole plot as she had heard it. Which wouldn't be a nice thing to do either. It was none of her business, and she would just forget it.

Then suddenly the sound of a great plane came nearer, and they all stood breathless, so that Diana's voice sang out quite clearly.

"There, I told you Teddy would come back in time for the first dance!"

But the big plane passed over the house toward the country club and did not even come low nor waver in its straight course across to the mountains, and a great disappointment came into Amory's heart, although but the instant before she had been quivering with dread lest he should have returned, and would try to be openly friendly with her.

When the plane had sailed far in the moonlight

and become a mere silver moth against the light, she looked down and saw John Dunleith and Diana Dorne just disappearing down the hemlock drive, and the other young people were nudging and whispering after them in wicked glee. Amory decided that this was the time for her to disappear, and was soon up in the safe shelter of her own room.

Sitting so by her window in the dark, with the great moon sailing over the mountains in the distance, and the cool dark lawn below where little nestling insects made sweet low sounds, and dew distilled the sunlight of the day into rare frail perfumes, Amory grew lonely. How was she to stand endless days like this all alone in a world of her own? If only the work would last in the evening too it would not be so bad, for then she could have no chance to think. But this having a beautiful leisure and no one to enjoy it with, was worse than no leisure at all. Of course there were books and she might light her reading lamp and read over the story of Gareth again. But somehow she felt too restless for reading to-night. Where was the Gareth now, to-night, who had told her to think of him by that name?

She knelt a long time by her window looking out into that pathless air through which he might be coming, and praying for him by the name he had told her to use, and yet there was an undertone of chiding in her heart that she was daring to do this for a stranger. She must look after her own thoughts and keep them to their right course!

The music had started downstairs now and floated sensuously out into the moonlight, calling in the young people who had drifted here and there about the grounds.

And up through the fringed hemlock drive came John Dunleith and Diana Dorne walking slowly together, the misty blue of her frock floating away from her little silver slippers like a wreath of frail fog. They came slowly, talking as they came, or rather, John Dunleith was talking, telling her about a mountain he had climbed, and the girl was listening, with white uplifted face, earnestly attending to what he was saying. How well she acted her part. If Amory had not heard her plan the horrid joke she never would have believed that this girl was not deeply enamored of the young man. A wave of disgust went over her once more that any girl could care to do the thing that this girl was doing. Would she really carry it out? And if she did what would be the outcome? Would her own heart perhaps become entangled? Or had she perhaps her own heart too well fortified to fall before a poor man's siege?

They came slowly and paused just below Amory's window.

"Oh," said the girl, "I must have dropped my shawl back there in the drive! Would you mind going back for it? I'm fearfully tired with all I've done to-day, and I'm afraid it will be ruined if it lies in the dew. It is embroidered white silk, with long fringe. You can't miss it. Would you mind? I'll just sit here by the window till you get back."

The young man went at once, down into the darkness again, and came back presently with the shawl, but walking more slowly, and standing afar off from the window, looking in.

Diana had disappeared inside, and the music was going now with all its might, an abandoned dance of the hour. Amory remembered the talk of the morning and doubted not that Diana had found some other partner to help her carry out her plan. But the young man with the long white fringe dripping from his hand, was not coming on toward the window, and she thought she heard a low whistle from his direction. Then a quick alert shadow moved out of the darkness and joined him, and they came nearer to the terrace.

"Kid, will you take this shawl in to Miss Dorne and make my apologies?"

"Aw, take it yerself, Pard. She don't like me fer little apples."

"It can't be done, Kid, not to-night. You'll have to help me out. I fished all the afternoon and now I've got to go and get ready to preach. Thanks, Kid, I knew you would!" and the man slipped away into the shadows.

Reluctantly the boy came up to the window and waited till a pause came in the music.

"Hey, Di," he called out rudely, "here's yer shawl. John said he hadta study now."

There was silence for a second while the whole gang of dancers took in the meaning of this message, and then a laugh rang out, mocking, and gay, and that would not be silenced.

"Hey, Di!" called some one as the laughter died away, "are you going to let the parson get away with that? Teddy and the parson both standing you up in one night? That's too much!"

CHAPTER VI

RISING from the green of the flying field, and curving about to face the girl he had just left behind him on earth, Gareth Kingsley had a sudden reluctance to go. He watched her standing there by the tall hedge with her hands outspread, and the background of the rugged castle behind her and felt it was a picture he would not soon forget. How sweet and unspoiled she was. How pretty she looked standing there against the dark of the hedge in her simple little blue frock. No frills and nonsense about her. No rouge and lipstick and affectations, just pure simple girl, with a light in her eyes and some sense in her head, and convictions about right and wrong.

It might be all very well for men to do as they pleased in these days when old limits were being torn down, but when it came to a woman, it was different. She was meant to be something sweet and fine, and when she wasn't there seemed to be no reason for her existence. His mother had been like that. He remembered her well, and her voice as she used to call him "Gareth." And this had been the first girl he had ever seen that he cared to have call him by that name.

He watched her as he came on and she stood, her eyes lifted, wonder glowing in her face. What beautiful eyes! And she didn't know it either. They were like a child's, pure crystal over that deep wonderful blue.

He could feel her little book pressing over his heart, for the pocket was a tight fit, and it somehow warmed his spirit to think she had given it to him, something of her very own that she was fond of, and enjoyed. A sudden desire seized him to leave something of his own with her, something to remind her of himself beyond that most chaste kiss he had left upon her fingers. He was coming toward her rapidly now. A moment more and she would be too far below unless he turned back again. He was not wont to turn back after he had started.

He seized the corner of the handkerchief that

fluttered from his pocket. He would throw that down. But there must be something to weight it, or it might fly into a tree top where she could never get it, or on top of the hedge where she would not even notice it.

Quickly he snatched off the silver wings that were pinned to his coat, had been there since the decoration had been given him, and knotted the corner of the silk about it, flinging it out just in time.

Did she see it? He watched eagerly. Yes, she had caught it. He waved another farewell—smiling down on her, the little sweet girl in the blue frock—and mounted up to the heavens, a kind of delicious exhilaration filling his veins.

What was this that possessed him, anyway? Was he turning foolish, that a single girl could make him happy like that just to look at her? Was he falling for a girl at last? His heart—! "Well, what of it?" his heart defiantly answered, and he laughed aloud with the engine as he rode along the sky.

What strange unusual questions she had asked. Well, perhaps he was to blame for her asking them. They were only in her eyes, and she had not really intended to speak them aloud.

Did he know God? Was he saved?

He recognized the phraseology as a kind of shibboleth of some religious order perhaps, with which he was unfamiliar. But the words held a strange arresting quality, and brought thoughts that he had never entertained before.

Being saved implied a possible danger. And of course, being a flier, he had always known in the back of his mind, that a flier sooner or later was doomed to fall. Somehow or other it got them all. But that it might get him he had never admitted even to himself. He had a feeling that if he even admitted such a possibility to himself he would be doomed.

But now he knew that the fact had been there in his mind all the time; admitted or not, it had crept in, and was established. All he could do was refuse to look the fact in the face and go gayly on as long as he held out. In fact that very program had been a kind of a code with him, a religion of the skies if one chose to call it so, a moral outfitting without which no man would dare leave the earth.

And now this girl had seemed to suggest that there was something more, something that he had left undone which would have put him where he had no need to fear, even if the worst came.

He had never lived in an atmosphere where eternity was considered a factor of life. Live your best and get what you could out of it, and then what would came, and it was liable to be pretty good after all. That was his creed, and the creed of those with whom he came into contact. On the whole he considered himself to be as good as most, a trifle better than some, and it had never troubled him. Now suddenly, imperatively his thoughts were arrested. The clear eyes of the girl had seen something else. She had read him keenly, he could see that. She had seen a lack. Well, maybe some time he would look into it. If a girl like that had seen something worth while in knowing a God, had thought it possible, it was worth at least looking into.

He sailed gayly off into the blue, breathing the clear air, delighting in the wideness about him, and in the power of his engine. He loved to fly. He had utmost confidence in his machine, in himself. That anything could happen was so remote a possibility that it did not figure on his horizon at all.

Traffic in the skies was not much congested that morning. He passed but one plane till he was within an hour of New York. He watched it cutting through the morning, noted its build and the way it was running, mentally placed it among the class of planes he knew, and sailed on.

He was flying over small towns now, and looking down he saw pleasant homes nestling along a cozy street, vines growing over porches, gardens glowing, children playing about, one sailed a miniature airplane into a tree. Nice little homes with brisk loving wives tidying up the front porch, or hanging little garments on a line. He had never paid much heed before to little homes like these. His life had been hedged about in mansions, with luxuries, but a little home like this one just below him would be pleasant with a girl like that one he had left behind in Briarcliffe. He had never seen a girl before that he had felt he would care to take to a little house and try to be happy with her there. Most of the girls he knew wanted a palace, and all that went with it, and somehow setting up a new one on his own account with any of the young women in his crowd had never yet appealed to him.

He was flying lower now, just to notice these pleasant homes. There was a woman coming out of one door with a baby in her arms, pushing a little coach down the steps ahead of her. She ought to be careful with a baby in her arms. Suppose she should fall down the steps. It was a tiny baby with a blue coat the color of the dress his girl wore that morning whein he had bade her good-by. It was—

Just then it happened—something indefinable about the sound of his engine. He turned his eyes sharply away from earth and gave strict attention to business.

But there was something wrong. And it wasn't any of the ordinary things that usually went wrong either. He knew that at the start. And now the engine had gone dead! The friendly roar that made things seem so all right had ceased! He must do something about it! What ought he to do? There was no open space down there below him. Just houses, cozy little homes, with children playing!—And the baby!— And the mother! Would the little girl in the blue dress remember to pray for him?—|

Two men stepped out of a rose arbor where they had been figuring by a table. They had pencils and note books in their hands and were looking up.

"Something must be the matter up there!" said the younger man. "See! His nose is pointing down! Look how low he is going—! How slow—! I never saw any one do anything like that! Why, that's dangerous! Marcella, take the baby in the house quick! There really ought to be some regulation about the air. People have no right—!"

"Oh, he's only doing some stunt," said the other man easily. "He'll right himself in a minute. See there! His nose is pointing up again!"

"But his engine isn't running. Listen! I heard when it stopped. That's what made me come out to look! And see! He's dropping again!"

"There, he's pointing the nose up again. See. He's only turning somersaults again or making circles or something!"

"He's crazy!" shouted the younger man. "Don't you see his tail is falling all the time? He couldn't do stunts with his engine shut off, could he?"

"Don't ask me! They do almost any queer thing in the skies nowadays."

Up in the air Gareth Kingsley was doing his best, trying this and that, the usual emergency acts that men of his profession are trained to know. But none of them worked! Steadily, slowly, like a feather on a sultry day the great bird was wavering toward the ground, and there were only little cozy houses, and children playing in the gardens, and a baby in a mother's arms, wherever he would land.

It was not so much the thought of himself wrecked, his unparalleled reputation as a flyer gone! It was not what would be his own future even. It was that somehow now his frenzied brain had conceived the idea that down there with the children in the little cozy yards, and with the mother and the baby, close under his ship, stood a little sweet, white-faced girl in a blue frock looking up at him with trusting eyes, unafraid, and praying.

The nose of his plane was pointing desperately downward now, and he spoke out loud;

"Oh, God! If you'll just right me now, I'll take time off as soon as I get to New York and try to find you!"

He was not aware that he was praying. He was working all the time, and now his desperate fingers touched some vital part of the machinery and suddenly the engine spoke. With a great sigh like a relieved prisoner, it spoke, then sighed, then roared, and bit hold of the air again. Gareth felt it quiver beneath him, felt the great bird rise, and knew that he was in control again. Up and up till the little village was safely far away, out and beyond and away from that place where God had stopped him on his way, he flew. What had been the matter he did not know. None of the reasoning that he had been taught fitted the facts. By all the laws of science he ought to be lying now a wreck on some of those little cottage roofs over there. If what had seemed to happen had been true, his engine could not of itself have righted itself.

If the fault had been in himself, some mental aberration, it had never happened before, and he could not account for it any more than he could account for some strange break in his machinery that had miraculously cured itself and gone on. But if it was his own mental breakdown that had caused that almost horrible accident, then he ought never to fly again.

As he went steadily, strongly on again into the morning, the trembling in his limbs slowly steadying, his confidence returning rapidly, his brain clearing keenly; he came to a conclusion. Whatever the immediate cause of that sudden cessation of machinery, whether actual or mental; whether it could ever be clearly demonstrated or not for the satisfaction of any who might learn of the happening; for himself he was satisfied that God had been calling his attention, and he knew that the vow he had made in the stress of his anxiety must be kept as soon as he reached his destination.

And now, as he drew a deep breath of thankfulness, and realized that he was really going on normally again, he understood that the safe thing to do would be to seek a good landing field where he could find a mechanic, and go over his machinery carefully before he progressed further. In his heart he did not believe that this was necessary. He felt in his spirit that the thing would not happen again until he was safely at his destination, nevertheless, he knew that he had no right to take chances after a warning like this, so he sought a field a few miles further ahead and went down.

It took some time to go carefully over every part, but conscientiously he let nothing escape, and finally satisfied that he had done all that the best flyer alive could do in like circumstances, he embarked and set sail once more.

It was late when he reached New York. The men he was to meet were impatient. They had made their plans, and they wanted him to be ready to start on his record setting hop the next morning. It mattered nothing to them that the next morning would be the Sabbath day. The better the day the better the deed. As his sponsors they felt the time was ripe for his particular stunt, and they would brook no delay.

Neither did the day mean anything to Gareth. But there was something on his mind.

"I'm not at all sure I can make it," he said firmly. "There is something I must do first."

"How long will it take you?"

"Why I can't tell that. It may take only an hour or two. I can't tell till I try."

"But couldn't someone do it for you! You know, Kingsley, it's important that we seize the right moment. Your act is the logical follow up of Norrington's trip last week, and we have information that makes it pretty sure the Boris Brothers are planning to do something along these same lines within a few days now. We've got to beat 'em to it, you know, or your goose is cooked!"

"Can't help it!" said Gareth pleasantly with his good natured grin. "This has got to be done first."

"But what's the nature of this duty? Can't you tell us? Maybe we can help hurry it up."

Gareth looked at them earnestly, those four hard headed business men, holding the purse strings tight, and opening the bag only to let more money in. He saw himself asking any one of those men how to find God. How could they help him? They did not know God themselves. They did not believe in Him. But he did, now! He knew there was a God and he meant to find Him before he did anything else. Never would he venture into the air again until he had within himself the talisman of which the little blue eyed Amory had told him.

So, though they urged, and bullied and bribed, he was firm, till they hurried him off at last and told him to make it snappy, that the world was waiting for his return, and thousands of dollars were hanging in the offing.

Gareth went out. He had no idea where he was going.

He stepped into a cheap little restaurant and swallowed a cup of bitter coffee, and then he started out on the street to find a church. Saturday afternoon, and the half holiday crowds out in full force. He was not familiar with churches in New York nor anywhere else, but his common sense told him that a church ought to be the place where he might find out about God. It did not occur to him that most churches were not open on Saturday afternoons.

But after walking blocks he did find a church, with its side door open, and stepping in he met a janitor.

"Yes, the minister's in," said the janitor. "He just came in to his study a while back to get a book or two. I don't think he's left yet, but I'm not so sure he can see you. He doesn't see callers afternoons usually, especially not Saturday afternoons. Have you an appointment? I could give him your name."

"No," said Gareth, "but you can tell him I won't keep him long. I just wanted to ask him a question or two."

"You're not an agent, are you? He won't see agents at all."

"No, I'm an aviator," laughed Gareth.

"Well, you wouldn't want me to tell him what you've come about, would you? So he might judge if he could see you to-day or not? Because he might want you to wait till Monday."

Now he was here Gareth felt a strange reluctance toward telling his errand to any but a man of God.

"I can't wait till Monday. I'm in a hurry, and it's

important. I must tell him myself what my errand is, and if he can't see me now I'll have to go to some one else."

At that the janitor trudged away, and presently came back and led Gareth through a hallway into a pleasant room nicely furnished and lined from floor to ceiling with books.

The minister was seated behind a big mahogany desk and when he saw Gareth's uniform, and his engaging grin he came quite out of his comfortable chair to meet him, for he had feared that after all his denials this must be another form of agent.

"I'm in a hurry," said Gareth as he sat down in the chair opposite the minister, "and perhaps you are. I'll come to the point at once. I'm an aviator, and I'm going on a trip within the next few hours. Something has made me feel I need God. I'm all at sea how to go about it, and I figured you'd be able to tell me in a few minutes just what I ought to do."

"Why, that's very commendable, my dear fellow," said the minister affably. It had been many a day since any one had come to him inquiring the way to God. "Very commendable indeed. What—ah, were you thinking of? Did you wish to connect yourself with our church before you start on your voyage? That could be done. We usually have our communion service every three months and we receive new members at that time. We had our usual communion service last Sunday, I regret to say, but of course, if there is special need of haste it could be arranged privately, say to-morrow, if you wish. Was that your idea?"

Gareth looked puzzled.

"No," he said, half hesitating, "I don't know anything about churches. I've never had much to do with them. I just want to get sort of acquainted with

God. A friend told me I ought to know God. She seemed troubled that I wasn't what she called 'saved.'"

"I see," said the minister, "you wish to take some sort of a stand on the Lord's side. That is very gratifying indeed. Very commendable! I suppose, my dear fellow, that you would perhaps like to have the ordinance of baptism administered. That is a simple matter of course, unless perhaps you have already been baptized?"

Gareth still looked puzzled.

"Do you mean was I christened? I don't believe I ever was. I never heard of it. I don't think it was a custom in our family. But what has that got to do with being saved?"

"Why, my dear fellow, we are told to believe and be baptized. Of course I do not mean to say that baptism is *necessary* to salvation. It is not exactly a *saving* ordinance, but it is the outward sign of course. I am taking it for granted that you believe?"

"I never have before," answered Gareth thoughtfully, "but something happened that made me sure I do. Of course I know absolutely nothing about this line, that's why I came to you."

"Well, then, my dear fellow, I would advise you to be baptized. We could arrange it to-morrow morning quietly before the service, here in my study if you prefer."

"But what is baptism for?" persisted the puzzled young man. "I've heard of it always, of course, but it never meant a thing in my young life."

"Why, baptism," said the minister deliberately, "is a symbol of the inward cleansing, the cleansing of your soul."

Gareth looked helpless.

"Is that all?" he asked. "Isn't there anything for me to *do?*"

It all seemed so hopelessly indefinite. It had not occurred to him that his soul needed cleansing. He had no sense of sin.

"Oh, of course, my dear fellow, there are the means of grace. Attendance on divine worship, reading of the holy scriptures, prayer, giving to worthy causes. Those are all helps to a life hid with Christ in God."

Gareth felt as if he were going in deeper and deeper and getting nowhere. Why couldn't the man use language he understood? But he assented helplessly. He had a wistful feeling that if only that little girl with the clear blue eyes were here, she would make it all plain. But she was not here and he must do the best he could and make haste about it.

It was arranged that Gareth was to receive the ordinance of baptism the next morning at ten o'clock. The minister did not feel that he could bring it about sooner as it was customary to have some member or members of his church present, and he felt sure he would not be able to reach any of them before the morning hour.

Gareth left the minister, half hesitating, feeling that he had done all he knew how to do, yet knowing there was a lack somewhere. If only he had asked Amory what she meant by being saved! She seemed to have some real definite idea back of her words, something that the old man with all his dignity did not seem to understand.

Perhaps it was her pure childlike faith in things unseen. But where did she get it? What had *she* got to rest it upon? The minister had talked in high sounding phrases that he had never heard before and got him nowhere. Why hadn't he asked the girl what she meant and how he could get it?

It was almost twilight when he went out into the street again. He looked uncertainly about him and felt dissatisfied. He wished he knew something more to do.

He went finally to a telephone booth and called up the four men who were his sponsors for the trip. He told them it was possible he might be able to start tomorrow noon, if the weather conditions were favorable. They grumbled a little but accepted his decision because they knew they had to do so. He was a young man who usually knew his own mind.

Five minutes later a paragraph for the last edition of the evening papers was telephoned to the Associated Press:

"Ted" Kingsley planning to hop off at noon tomorrow! Bound for Siberia via Alaska.

CHAPTER VII

GARETH went to a hotel and ate his dinner. Then instead of hunting up some friends for a jolly evening as he would naturally have done at another time, he went to his room and took out the little book. He felt he had a duty to perform, a problem to work out which somehow might be solved by that book.

He opened the book to the fly leaf first and read the neat inscription:

AMORY LORRIMER
From Mother,
For my dear little girl on her fifth birthday

There followed a date and the name of a town which the young man never heard of; below was written in a cramped little-girl hand "Mother dear went home to heaven"—and another date a year and a half later than the first.

The young man's eyes clouded with tears. So this book that he had so lightly begged from her was a treasure, a precious memorial of a beloved mother. A link between her little girlhood and her present life. He could hardly remember his own mother. For a moment he thought perhaps he should send it back to her at once, and then he remembered her eyes as she had said gravely:

"I *want* you to have it." No, he would not return it. He wanted to read it first. But he would take it back to her on his return, or, if anything happened to him they would send the little book to her. He would see to that. He would keep it in an addressed envelope in his pocket while he flew, so that if he was wrecked the book might stand a chance of finding her again. And that this might not fail he went at once before he had looked further into its pages, and addressed one of the hotel envelopes to Miss Amory Lorrimer at Briarcliffe. When he had stamped it with more than enough to carry the book he went back to his reading.

He discovered that there were marked verses, and sometimes marked chapters. One said in fine little printing: "I learned this chapter on my tenth birthday."

Another was marked, "The verse my mother loved," and still another, "A verse I love to think about."

Bit by bit he gathered up a picture of her life, this sweet child whom he had come upon so unexpectedly and seen but for a few minutes, and when he read the verses she had marked, he seemed to be looking into her soul, and seeing things in the book as she had seen them. It seemed to open an amazing new world to him. He had not dreamed there was a girl in the world who lived in the thought of God in this intimate way.

Skipping through the book from one marked verse to another he came on some amazing facts about God as revealed in Christ, and when at last he lay down to rest he carried the little book with him and slept with it in his hand. He had a strange feeling that his experience in the clouds that morning had changed the whole of life for him, yet he had as yet no definite idea of what it might be going to mean.

The service in the dim old historic church the next morning seemed strange to him. The empty pews, the distant music as the organist played softly in preparation for the day, the few solemn-faced strangers who assisted the minister, the stately words that were pronounced, some of which he recognized to have read the night before out of Amory's little book, the drops of water on his brow, his name "Gareth" and "Child of God, I baptize thee in the name of the Father, and of the Son, and of the Holy Ghost!"

Saved! Was he saved? Had this ceremony somehow mysteriously put upon him the mark of God?

He went forth into the street in a kind of awe, trying to realize that some mysterious change had taken place. He was God's now. His seal had been put upon him. He did not in the least understand what nor why, but he was willing to believe it was so as the minister had said, and as he had read in the book in several places. He believed because he had met God out there in the air, and had made a covenant with Him—he called it a bargain—and He had accepted that covenant and brought him safe to New York. That part was simple enough. The rest was spiritual and he could not understand it. He did not know why any one thought he understood it. But he was glad the matter was settled so far as he could settle it.

He went straight to the office where he had met the four men yesterday who were his sponsors. There was yet an hour to high noon when he was supposed to set sail. He was keeping his appointment, while church chimes were ringing on the Avenue, and the world was just beginning to waken.

But the barometric conditions were not favorable for starting yet. He must wait. Perhaps at midnight— He went back to his hotel impatiently— Now that he had done his best to fulfill his promise he was anxious to be off. He wanted to get back and talk with Amory. But since he must wait it was necessary that he sleep and store up strength for his flight. So to sleep he went, and did not waken till almost sundown. After a light supper he went out for a walk. The weather seemed to have changed for the better. His thoughts leaped up with relief. Probably he could get off by midnight after all. How he longed to get this trip over with. He had never been so impatient before over anything he had ever tried to do. And yet, somehow, it was as if an unseen hand was detaining him, holding him back from starting, even if the barometer had been right. It was as if there was still something left undone, some condition not yet complied with.

He did not notice where he was going, turning a corner here or there, wherever the traffic was least congested. There were bells ringing again, Sabbath bells, evening bells, calling across a work-worn sin-harried city, a call of prayer. Something wistful in his soul was listening to them and answering, longing to find the satisfaction and sense of safety, of which he had never before felt the need in his self-satisfied young life.

Suddenly he halted before a great sign in front of an old gray church. The sign stood out level with the sidewalk, and announced in mammoth letters that there was a Bible Conference inside that church. But it was not in the Bible Conference that Gareth was interested. It was in the two lines that stood out in still larger letters below the heading: "WHAT SHALL I DO TO BE SAVED?" and below it: "YE MUST BE BORN AGAIN!"

It startled him to have his own question staring at him in great red and black letters. And that queer answer, "Ye Must Be Born Again!" What did it mean? How could a man be born again? But perhaps it was not an answer. Why shouldn't he go in and see?

The door of the church stood open. It was early and there was no one inside but the janitor. Gareth approached him and asked about the service, and what the sign meant. Was that the speaker's subject?

The janitor assured him that is was and that the speaker was most unusual.

"It's early," he said reassuringly, "but you was wise to come early. This morning every seat was full, and some sat on the pulpit steps. It's liable to be worse to-night. Everybody's crazy about this preacher."

Gareth sought out a seat under the gallery, and sank into it with relief. There was something restful about the very atmosphere in here away from the din of the street. The lights, save one by the door, were not yet turned on, and he sat looking about in the dusk at the rows of pews, and the great stained glass windows which gave forth faint colors from the twilight outside.

Gradually people stole in and sat down, bowing their heads in prayer. Gareth sat with a new kind of awe stealing over him, and a sense that there were other people seeking God as well as himself.

Presently the lights sprang up and the church began to fill. The organ played softly, and brisk men walked into the pulpit, several of them, all with strong faces, who looked as if they lived near to real things. There was singing that bore along like a strong tide, surprised him with its earnestness, and thrilled him with its sweetness, though many of the voices were not cultured. There was a tender earnest appeal in it.

The man who finally stood up to speak, with a limp-covered open Bible in his hand, had a face that arrested his attention at once. It was alert and true with a settled peace about it and he spoke like one with authority, in a cultured, scholarly voice, yet quiet and most arresting. Gareth was not fond of listening to addresses, yet this man held his attention from start to finish, and it seemed when he was done as if he had been speaking only about five minutes.

Gareth learned for the first time that since Adam's sin all men were born spiritually dead, and could not understand spiritual things until they were born again. He learned that salvation was not to be bought, nor won by anything that a man could do, which much astonished him; that it was a free gift of grace. He learned that the only thing a man had to do was to accept that gift by believing on the Lord Jesus Christ and His atoning death on the cross to cover his own sin, and that the moment he believed he was born again and became a child of God.

The speaker substantiated every statement he made by reading from the Bible. The simple explanation, the beauty and easiness of the plan of salvation was startlingly within the reach of the most ignorant. Several times the preacher quoted the verse, "He that believeth on the Son *hath* everlasting life!" If that were true, he could go forth out of this church knowing that he was a child of God, and his salvation secure. Was this what Amory had meant?

The prayer that followed the sermon seemed to set his own immediate case before the eyes of the Most High God, and he found himself with bowed head, as it were standing before the God who had met him in the air, listening to the plea of Jesus the Saviour who had given His own life that this salvation might be his.

When the service was over he stood for an instant looking at the strong face of the preacher, wishing he might ask him a few questions; but there was already an eager crowd around him, so Gareth went out into the street and made his way to his hotel.

It was growing late. If conditions were as he felt they were likely to be, there would be nothing in the way of his starting soon. There was a strange peace upon him. The restlessness of the morning was gone. A new exhilaration had taken its place. There were still things he did not understand, things he was taking for granted, but something strange and wonderful had been done for him, and he trod the city streets like one who had just been introduced to God.

When he reached his hotel room he walked over to the telephone and stood for some minutes looking at it. Then he called up long distance and got his aunt's home in Briarcliffe.

When the butler tapped upon Amory's door and told her some one wished to speak to her on the telephone she arose with such haste that she dropped the book she was reading, and almost tripped over the rug as she reached the door. What was wrong at home? Was Aunt Hannah worse? Surely nothing short of something tragic would make Aunt Jocelyn waste the price of a long distance telephone call? Money was too precious just now.

It seemed a mile down the stairs, and down the long hall to the telephone booth, and she felt weak as she drew the door shut after her, and slid into the seat with the receiver in her hands.

"Hello! Is that you, Miss Lorrimer?" came a strong voice with a lilt in it.

Now who could that be? It wasn't any of the boys at home, nor yet the next door neighbor who was the only near neighbor that had a telephone where Aunt Jocelyn would be likely to resort in time of stress.

"Hello!" she said. "Yes," in such a weakly little voice that the question came again.

"Is that you, Miss Lorrimer? Amory?"

And then she knew and a thrill came to her heart. It was Gareth! Gareth for whom she had prayed all day long. He was alive then! He had not flown as the family had said he was to do!

"Oh, yes," she said, but still her voice was husky with feeling. "Yes, this is Amory."

"Speak a little louder. I can't hear you."

"Yes, this is Miss Lorrimer. This is Amory!" and found her lips were trembling and her voice was laughing out in triumph, "Shall I—shall I call some one else?"

"Not on your life, little girl!" came back the hearty answer. "It's *you* I want to talk to. This is Gareth."

"Oh-h!" rippled Amory happily, "Yes— *Gareth!*"

"That's the talk, little girl. Well, I'm hopping off, and I had a sneaking notion you wouldn't mind if I said good-by—once more!"

"Oh!" said the girl with suddenly frightened eyes. "Oh, then you're really going?"

"Yes."

"When?"

"In a couple of hours."

"Oh!" There was a choking sound in the girl's voice.

"You won't forget what you promised?"

"Oh, no—I have—been—*remembering!*"

The words came hesitantly.

"I thought so!" he said reverently. "But that's another story. I just wanted you to know that if anything happens it's all right with me the way you said. In any case—I'll—meet you again—*in the morning!*" There was a queer little satisfied ring of a laugh in his voice, yet it was a reverent laugh.

"Oh!" she said with a choking sound to her voice again as if the tears were coming, "Oh, I'm glad! But—don't you want me to call—some one else—!"

"I certainly do *not!* This is just for you, see? Keep it absolutely under your hat. Understand? Good-by—" his voice trailed off chokily, "Dar—!"

Was that "Darling" he had said? "Good-by, darling!" A beautiful pain stabbed through her heart, and the tears were dropping on her hands. She stared around the little booth with wide eyes, the receiver shook in her hand, and her senses seemed to have deserted her. Then a sudden wild fear seized her and she cried:

"Oh— Are you there?"

What she had been going to say if he was there she did not know, but the silence frightened her.

"Are you there?" she repeated trying to control her voice to its natural sound. But there came no answer over the wire. The other end had hung up!

Presently she gathered strength to hang up her receiver, and slip guiltily out of the booth and up the stairs, thankful only that no one came in her way, and she might get back to the sanctuary of the darkness and her own room without having to speak to any one.

She locked her door and dropped on her knees beside the window with only the stars looking down, put her hands on her hot, hot cheeks, and then buried her face on her folded arms.

"Darling! Darling!" came the echo of that soft last word, so low she was not sure she had heard it at all. Oh, how bold, how dreadful she was to even imagine it. What should she do with her heart to keep it from leaping in this unnatural crazy way! And why should she think about whether he had said it or not when he had told her before the most wonderful thing in the world? He had told her that he was safe, whatever came he was safe! That meant that a wonderful change had come to him somehow. That meant that her prayers had been answered.

A wave of gladness surged over her, made up of fear and joy and hope, and still that soft word chimed over in her heart, "Darling! Darling! Darling!"

Gareth had hung up the receiver quickly and stood, his eyes full of starry lights, a smile of daring on his lips! He had not meant to say that—Darling!—He breathed it softly again, and was glad he had said it. Perhaps she had not heard it. He had hung up quickly because he had not meant that word to be heard. But now he was glad he had said it.

He stood a moment staring down at the telephone, smiling. Then with a grave look coming over the smile on his lips he stepped to the middle of the room and looked up.

"God,—I'm depending—on you—to—see me—through!"

His eyes were wide as if he were looking straight into the face of the Almighty, and the light on his face was good to see. Then he turned and went out of the room and downstairs to his taxi.

An hour later he stood on the flying field beside his plane ready for his trip. Everything had been gone over, his engine was in fine trim, nothing had been forgotten. The moon was high and bright, the barometer promised good weather, and he was impatient to be off.

Around him gathered in a group were the reporters, a couple of enterprising photographers who had just snapped a few flashlight pictures, and the four men who were backing him. A bunch of mechanicians eyed him jealously, and he flashed them one of his smiles that the newspapers raved about, but his thoughts were with a little girl whose voice had sounded choked with tears. He had just thought of something. She wouldn't cry if she didn't care, would she? She wouldn't, would she? Darling! The darling little girl! Why hadn't he met her sooner? If he had he might not be trailing off on this fool expedition now. Who cared whether a plane could go to Siberia by way of Alaska or not? Why should anybody care? Darling! Darling! Darling! A chime of bells in his heart!

"Contact?"

"Contact!"

The engine spoke, throbbed, the great bird rose into the silver sea of the air, and he was off.

They watched him a moment till he was a mere speck in the moonlight, and then they hurried off to get his picture in the morning papers.

CHAPTER VIII

SABBATH at Briarcliffe had not been a restful day.

To begin with there had been a match between two world-famed golf players, at the country club, and the young people trooped downstairs noisily, much earlier than under any other consideration they could have been induced to arise. But early as they were they did not get down in time to see John Dunleith and eat breakfast with him. Only Neddy had that honor. Both Neddy and John were gone long before the golfers put in an appearance.

"I'm going to Sunday School with John," explained Neddy when his sister wanted him to play a set of tennis singles with her so she would keep in good form. "John hasta teach a class, an' we havta be there early." He spoke with importance as if his duties as attendant on his cousin were of the nature of a religious ceremony.

"Great Cats!" said Doris, twisting her lips into a grimace of contempt. "Run right along then, Buddy, and don't soil your hands."

Diana came down a little later than the rest, having attained a costume suited either to the country club or an elaborate church affair. It had taken her some time to decide upon it, but it was as effective in its way as the fishing costume had been, and every bit as costly. White dress so simple and so ravishing that any woman would have known it could only be achieved by one of the great dressmakers of Paris. White shoes, and a wide brimmed white hat with a single great white velvet rose poised on its brim. A white and golden girl she was, and strangely her eyes had gold lights in them too. Lovely eyes that could tantalize and yet could look so genuine.

Amory had her breakfast in the sunny breakfast room by herself for everybody else ate in the big dining room. It was the only place where there was room enough for the party.

Amory had inquired of Christine concerning churches. She had a fancy to hear John Dunleith preach, but Christine had no idea which church it might be.

"There's the Episcopal, of course, that's the big lovely church about a quarter of a mile up the road. But he's not there I'm sure for he doesn't wear the collar for it. And there's the Presbyterian Church a little farther on, but it's quite the richest church outside the Episcopal. I'd not think he'd be preaching there. There's a Baptist over at Raleigh Heights that they say is much liked, and there's a Methodist up the road the other way that has more members than any church around, they are quite fine churches, but I can't say which it is would have him. Though he does seem a nice young man. But I'm sure if he were at all great Madam would have made them all go to church, and there's not one of them started as far as I can see.

"Of course there's the chapel, down in the village," added Christine as a second thought. "He might be even there."

Amory decided to try the chapel. She would likely find it if she walked long enough, and at least she would find some service some where to break the monotony of the dull day in the great strange house. She was not used to having Sunday just like any other day: It made her quite unhappy. The name chapel sounded as if there might be a simple service that would seem more homelike than any of the other churches described. So Amory took her quiet way down the long drive, and out the wooded gateway, into the road where she had arrived but a few short days before.

Diana lay in the lounging chair on the terrace and watched her go with narrowing eyelids and thoughtful mien. Presently she dismissed Fred and a youth named Clarence who were hovering around her anxious to be of service, saying she wanted to write some letters and might come to the country club later. She slipped into the house, but emerged as soon as the young men were out of sight, and looking stealthily about to make sure no one saw her, she followed the path that Amory had taken. She was thinking perhaps that John Dunleith had told Amory where he was going to preach. Leave it to Diana to think out a way!

She was carrying a worn but expensively bound little prayer book. It did not fit the chapel to which she was going, of course, but she did not know that, and it fitted the rôle she was playing, what did it matter? She had found it deep in a lower shelf of the library the night before, having hunted it out for the occasion.

In due time Amory arrived at the chapel which Christine had sketchily described, and was further assured by seeing the bulletin board in front which announced: "The Rev. John Dunleith will preach all this month."

The children were pouring out of the Sunday School as she arrived, but they did not go away, and presently turned and went back in again as if they loved it, hurrying to get seats.

Amory slipped through the young throng and took

a seat in a corner near the back. She would rather see than be seen. She felt strange and lonely. But a plain woman in a rusty black gown reached out a friendly hand and smiled, another woman handed her a hymn book and said it was a pleasant day, and somehow her frozen little self felt happier about going to church in a strange place.

There was scarcely an interval after she was seated until a wheezy little organ up in front began to play, and the congregation rose and sang with a will.

It was not until the sermon had begun that Diana Dorne came daintily in, pausing in the doorway, a lovely picture, clasping the worn prayer book in her hands. Diana certainly knew how to get herself up. There was a soft flush on her cheeks put there by skillful fingers, and the golden lights in her eyes played wistfully from under the golden fringes. Four men were instantly on their feet offering their seats, and Diana smiling graciously, accepted one from the best looking man, though it required five people to arise to let her in. She swept the congregation with a sweet deprecatory look that apologized publicly and bounteously for having disturbed their worship. She gave the impression of an earnest worshiper, found late through no fault of her own.

When the little hush occasioned by her coming had ceased, the voice of the preacher was heard once more but Diana lifting her golden gaze saw to her chagrin that he did not seem to have noticed her entrance at all. He was talking earnestly, quietly, without a particle of self consciousness or awkwardness, as if he had something of the utmost importance to tell.

As on the fishing expedition the day before, she discovered that she did not figure at all in his calculations. She was as it were as if she were not. Her lovely Paquin costume, and Lanvin hat were all wasted on him. They were wasted on this audience too, she perceived as she looked around her. No one was looking her way any longer, in spite of the disturbance she had made getting seated. There were girls of her own age there, dressed in flimsy silk or simple cotton frocks, with cheap little hats and strings of glass beads, who cast no envious eyes toward her. Not even the handsome young fellow who had given her his seat was looking at her now. He was standing back by the door because there was no other vacant seat, and he was earnestly listening to the preacher. They were all listening as if their lives depended on it. What could he be saying that interested them all so much? She set herself to listen also. Surely the poor nutty cousin from out west could not have anything important to say. Of course he was good looking, and rather intriguing, but these people did not look as if they were so much interested in *him*, in his personality, as they were in his theme.

When Diana at last settled down to really listen she tuned in on the most extraordinary sentence. It almost seemed as if he were directing it straight to her own thoughts, for she had been preening herself on her lovely white garments, and wishing he would look up and see how well she was looking, how fitly dressed for the day and the service.

"And the fine linen is the righteousness of the saints." That was the startling thing he was saying. She looked down quickly at the Paquin creation she was wearing. Of course a man wouldn't know its lovely dull sheen was silk, not linen. But surely, he was not talking to her, there in public, about her gown! Yet he said it in that quiet conversational tone just as he spoke when he sat fishing. It arrested her attention.

"The fine linen," went on the clear quiet voice, "is

God's righteousness put upon our moral nakedness
to cover it from sight forever. Christ has cleansed us
by His blood, and then put this lovely garment of
His righteousness about us to fit us to come into the
presence of God."

Diana suddenly shivered under her pretty white
silk, and her self-centered soul shrank within her.
The presence of God! Why did he want to talk about
a terrible thing like that? This was a glorious day.
He had been speaking of a lovely dress, and then he
mentioned the presence of God in the same breath!
Moral nakedness! What a phrase that was! What an
extraordinary person he was anyway! This was no
country gawk, no ignorant fanatic. This was a man
with a brain, a man who could use words, and hold
people!

She looked around upon the rapt company. Poor
old women with toil-worn hands and threadbare garments, giddy young girls, young men from all walks
in life, older men, business men, all listening as if
their very life depended upon his word.

And now he began to speak of One who was coming pretty soon, a bridegroom, of nobility perhaps,
coming for His bride. It sounded like a story, but
she could not quite get the thread of it. Was that the
little Whitney secretary sitting over in the opposite
corner? The bold creature! Was she presuming to
follow around a nephew of the house? Yet, of course,
Mrs. Whitney had rather discounted him, and had
placed this girl by his side at dinner. How she was
listening! She would be good looking if she had a
little more style! Had John Dunleith asked her to
church?

She shot another quick look at Amory, and was
puzzled by the sweet attention in her face. When she
turned back her giddy mind to the sermon again the
minister was speaking of one who was to stand upon

the Mount of Olives, and something in the way he said, "It may be very soon now," reminded her of what Mrs. Whitney had said about this young man having queer notions about the end of the world.

Diana's eyes narrowed and she studied him through her golden fringes, with a queer jealous pang at her heart. She felt that she must begin to get in some real personal work that very afternoon. She could not be balked in public this way, having the whole house party jeering at her whenever she failed to bring the young minister to time. She must learn not to boast. That was a bad move, last night, when she had sent him for her shawl, and he had returned it through Neddy, right before them all.

And suddenly she saw Neddy sitting up in the front seat, with a dignity that sat queerly on his remarkably clean chubby face. He was actually listening too, with round eyes of real interest. And in a flash she knew that she herself must be interested in what the minister had to say or she would never find a point of contact.

So she set herself to listen intelligently, and found herself astonished again at the words of wisdom he was speaking, words that searched her and pierced the shallowness of her soul, so that she was relieved when the service came to a close.

They sang a queer hymn at the end. They all burst forth into it like a triumphant shout. Some one gave her a book, and she read the words:

> "Jesus may come to-day,
> Glad Day! Glad Day!"

What did they mean? It must be that end of the world stuff. What a shame that such an interesting young man should be touched with a queer fanatical cult like this! Perhaps she could help to save him from such things and bring him back to normal once more. He seemed to have good common sense in other ways, and he certainly was a gentleman! She would see what she could do!

When the service was over she stepped back into the far end of the pew and waited, looking toward the pulpit and watching John Dunleith, smiling and trying to catch his eye across the crowds.

The people were pressing up around him, shaking his hand, smiling and some of them actually weeping through their smiles as if they were happy tears. Neddy stood close by him with an important little air of ownership about him, and basked in the smiles that were left over from the worship of his idol.

She must cultivate Neddy. Candy would do it. All boys loved candy! For at any cost she must win her wager that she had so lightly made, to subjugate this young man to herself. It was a new thing for her to have to work hard to get any young man to her feet.

So she stood and waited for him near the church door, watching him interestedly, showing him as plainly as she could that she was waiting there for his escort.

Once she looked with a quick searching eye to the corner where Amory had been sitting to see if the other girl waited also, but Amory had slipped out as soon as the service was over and was half way home by this time.

Diana had not seen the hostile eyes of Neddy, as he caught sight of herself. Neither did she hear the quick caught breath, and the low spoken word:

"Aw Gee! Let's beat it, Pard! The enemy's got an ambush!"

But John Dunleith had not needed the warning. He knew when the exquisite golden girl had entered. He knew, too, how little she had heard of what he had tried to say, and even though he had no eyes in the back of his head he knew that she was standing now, with that expectant expression on her face waiting for him to come out. His mind was working on the idea even as he answered the questions of the eager ones who wanted to know more about what he had told them that morning.

A sweet old lady in a gray dress and a little gray hat that suited her face but was not at all stylish slipped into the seat in front of where Diana stood waiting, and took her astonished and reluctant hand warmly.

"We're glad to see you here, my dear!" she said tenderly. "If you don't mind my saying it, you look like a white flower yourself. I was watching you while the minister was talking and I couldn't help thinking you looked as if you were wearing that white linen of Christ's righteousness that he talked about. I felt as if I just wanted to slip over here and put my fingers on your pretty dress and see if it was linen!"

The old lady put out a frail, gloveless finger and just touched the silk of Diana's Paris frock lightly.

Diana stared at her and said stiffly.

"Oh! Really! How amusing!"

"You'll be the minister's young lady, I'm thinking!" added the little old lady. She looked at her wistfully and passed out. Diana stared after her for an instant and then, turning back toward the pulpit, she saw to her vexation that John Dunleith and Neddy had utterly disappeared from the church!

How could they have got out?

There was a small narrow door at one end of the loft where the choir sat. They must have gone through that!

She gave a quick glance about the almost deserted church again, and hurried out. She would at least get a little ahead of them and then walk slowly so that they would have to overtake her. That would really be more interesting anyway, to show that she had not waited for them.

But the two she sought were not anywhere in sight, and the little door that seemed to open out of the choir loft at the left of the chapel was closed tight.

She hurried on a few steps, looking ahead and behind, and when she had gone a little farther she saw the man and the boy taking great strides across a field to her right in the direction of the woods. They would skirt the village, and come by a roundabout way to the house without ever coming near her! They had circumvented her again! And all that taunting crowd of guests would be out on the terrace when she reached the house, ready to laugh at her again. Diana Dorne coming back from *anywhere* unescorted. She set her lips! That must not be!

Swiftly she walked now, getting over the road in quick time till she came to the entrance of the country club, where after a hasty survey of the landscape, she turned in. Yes, there were some couples from the Whitney house still playing tennis. That was Susanne's cherry silk blouse. And off at the ninth hole was a girl in an orange and black sweater. That would be Caroline, and the two men with her would be Freddy, and Clarence. She drew a breath of relief remembering that she had told them she would come over perhaps when she finished her letters. There was no one about to say whether she had been at church or not. The day was saved!

Half an hour later she came sauntering back to the terrace where the rest of the guests were beginning to assemble. She was attended by three admiring young men, Freddy, and Clarence and Barry Blaine who had arrived that morning, presumably the substitute for the flier nephew who had disappeared.

Amory was watching from her window. She heard them call the newcomer Barry. He was thin and dark and rather wicked looking, she thought, as she studied him from behind her curtain.

The talk was excited, all about "Teddy." Some one had bought a Sunday paper and seen the announcement of the proposed flight.

"I think it was pernicious of him to go off like that without giving us the slightest hint of what he was going to do. Think of it! To be related to a real thrill like that and not be allowed the slightest particle of glory! We might have given a farewell dance at the country club!"

"I certainly am worried about him!" said Mrs. Whitney, coming out with the paper in her hand, and gazing sorrowfully at the flashlight picture of Gareth's best grin, taken standing by his plane. "It certainly is foolhardy of him to take another trip like that! Think of the anxiety of waiting to hear! I got a great many gray hairs the last trip he took. I can't see why he isn't satisfied with the laurels he has already won, without undertaking such an uninteresting trip as this. Who wants to go to Siberia by way of Alaska anyway? It's ridiculous. And such terribly cold places too. He'll be liable to get pneumonia! At least he could have postponed it, when I told him how much I wanted him for this party!"

"Oh, Poppycock!" said Mr. Whitney coming out behind her, "Ted will come through all right. He always does, doesn't he? And if Ted likes that kind of thing why that's the kind of thing he likes! Why worry? It's his life, not yours!"

"Well, I do worry!" persisted Mrs. Whitney. "I am the nearest to a mother he has left on earth. I mean to telegraph him not to go! I certainly shall! I'll tell him it's inexcusable to leave me this way when I was depending on him—!"

"But Barry is here, Mamma, you forget!" laughed Caroline. "You'll have to get some other reason."

"Oh, but I'm sending for Mary Lou Westervelt, that will make even couples again. I certainly shall assert my authority, and tell him he must give up this foolhardy flight. He has done enough for the world, and he owes his family a little now."

"Fat chance you'll have stopping that bird!" said her husband puffing away at a long black cigar. "You ought to have begun to exercise your 'authority' as you call it about fifteen years ago."

Amory had been requisitioned for the midday meal, and she was wishing she need not go down. She felt utterly out of harmony with the spirit of the other people. Not that it mattered much, for of course she would talk to nobody except the minister who would likely be seated next to her again. But there was so little they could talk about in a crowd like that. For instance, she would like to ask him some questions about his morning sermon, but they would scarcely fit where all the worldly banter was flying about. It would be like exposing sacred things to profane eyes. Perhaps there would be a chance for her to ask her questions some time later in the day when others were not about. She really had been deeply stirred by the sermon. She wondered what authority he had for some of the things he had said, whether they were generally accepted by Bible students, or whether they were fancies of his own which had no real foundation. He looked like a man who knew what he was talking about, and who would not say a thing unless he was sure it was true.

She hovered near the window until there came the call to dinner, and not till then did she see John Dunleith and Neddy approaching slowly through the garden, as if they had come from the woods. She knew Diana saw them, too, though she was apparently deeply absorbed in a gay conversation with the new dark young man, who looked at her with devouring eyes.

Dinner was even more unpleasant than she had feared, John Dunleith was indeed by her side, but he got almost no opportunity to speak to her during the entire meal, for strangely enough the girl Susanne was sitting on his other side, and she chose, whether from intention or from whim, to talk to him every minute. Her subject was the morning golf match between two noted golf players. She began by addressing him by name and asking him if he had seen it. And when he answered by a quiet negative, she went on to describe every play in detail, in the most extravagant terms giving her opinion of each player's ability. It was practically a recital for the grave and almost preoccupied young man had no opportunity to say anything but yes and no, although his abstracted air was little encouragement to her chatter.

Amory began to wonder, and finally to be convinced that there was some concerted action among the young people, for she noticed that Diana turned an annoyed look at Susanne occasionally in the intervals of her talk with Barry, and that the others cast occasional knowing glances toward Susanne and her new protégé. Later she overheard Susanne explaining to Barry on the terrace, before the others came out, that they were all combining to give Diana a rest from the burden she had undertaken, and Barry looked across the garden to where John Dunleith stood talking to Neddy and glared. But when Susanne asked him if he would join the combination and help, he said snappily: "You bet I will!"

"But don't tell Diana," laughed Susanne. "She never likes to be helped, you know."

"What do you take me for?" answered the dark young man with a sneer, and walked away to find Diana.

CHAPTER IX

BUT it happened that he went in the wrong direction, for Diana was strolling behind the garden hedge on the edge of the flying field quite out of sight, apparently hunting for a lost string of beads that might happen to be there as well as anywhere else, and listening through the hedge to the conversation between Neddy and the minister.

"No, son, we don't go fishing on the Lord's day," the young man was saying pleasantly, "but how about strolling down to the woods and having a story out of my Book? There's some grand stuff in that Book, son, and I have a hunch you'll like it."

"Aw' right!" agreed Neddy in a somewhat disappointed tone. Yet anything with Cousin John was interesting, he had found.

So they strolled through the garden gate, and out on the flying field, and there was Diana right on the job, and, looking up at exactly the right minute with a surprised expression, followed by one of relief and eagerness.

"Oh Heck!" said Neddy pausing sullenly. "Can you beat it? Now she'll tag along again. I'm gonta beat it!"

But John Dunleith took the lad's arm in a firm grip. "Stay right where you are, Pard, this is *your* afternoon!" he said in a low tone, and took his steady way as if to pass the girl.

"Oh, Mr. Dunleith," said Diana eagerly, "I've been so anxious to speak to you."

John Dunleith paused, half turning back toward her, his grip on Neddy's arm still firm. He lifted his eyebrows pleasantly and said, "Yes?" with a question mark, but with no invitation in his eyes for her to proceed to walk with them.

"I wanted to ask you about what you said this morning. I don't know that I fully understood all that you said."

"About what point, Miss Dorne?" he spoke crisply as though he had only a moment to stay, and pushing back his coat sleeve consulted his wrist watch unobtrusively.

Diana had not expected to be brought so suddenly to the point and she hesitated embarrassedly:

"Why—I— You said— That is—" she began, and then looking up at him sweetly propounded a question:

"Is it really true that you think the end of the world is coming very soon?" she asked plaintively. "Was that what you meant?"

"Was that what you got out of my talk this morning?" he asked, looking her gravely in the eyes.

"No, I—didn't know. They said that you—" began Diana in confusion.

"Oh! I see!" said the young man reflectively.

"I thought perhaps you would make it a little plainer," said Diana trying to speak brightly.

He looked down at her quizzically, almost sadly.

"If I thought you really wanted to know," he said, "of course I could. I wasn't talking about the end of the world, though. That is an entirely different matter. That will be a very terrible time. I was speaking this morning of the return of the Lord Jesus which will be a glad day for all His own."

"Oh, do you mean something like—Christmas?" she hesitated prettily with her handsome brows puckered as if trying to understand.

He wondered if it were possible that she was as ignorant as she seemed, and he gave her an inscrutable look but he answered her patiently.

"No, nothing like that. Have you a Bible?"

"Why, I did have one. We were obliged to have one at school, you know."

"I see. Well, I would advise you to read up about this if you are interested. I could give you a list of passages to look up."

"Oh, would you? That would be so kind!" exclaimed Diana in her sweetest tone. She had her back turned to the garden gate. She did not see Barry standing there glaring over it at her, nor hear Susanne's giggle in the offing. She gurgled on in her character of ingénue, white dress, white shoes, gold hair, earnest seeking blue eyes raised to the young preacher's face; a face that was strangely unmoved by the picture. "I'd be so much obliged for your help. But I've always had a lot of difficulty in understanding the Bible. Don't you think it is rather deep, Mr. Dunleith? Don't you think, really, that it might have been written in simpler language? I mean for ordinary persons like myself? The language sounds so stilted and unnatural. Don't you think so?"

"The Bible says about itself that the way of salvation is made so plain that the wayfaring man though a fool need not err therein," answered the preacher with that same quizzical smile that he had used before. It maddened her, but she kept her poise.

"Oh, dear me! Well, it really must have been my fault then, I suppose. I was a very giddy girl, I'm afraid, when I was in school, and of course I haven't read it much since. But I can come and ask you if I find anything that I do not understand? I am sure from having heard you this morning that you know a great deal about it. You preached so beautifully. I enjoyed it so much."

He gave her another of those quick looks, that almost seemed like a mingling of merriment and sadness, and she noticed that he did not thank her, but ignored her praise as if she had not spoken the words. He really was a strange young man. She could not reach him in the least through his own pride.

"I will give you some books that will help you if you are really in earnest," he went on. "If you want to understand the whole story you need to begin by knowing when sin began and what salvation means. Suppose you begin by reading the sixth chapter of Romans."

"Oh, really!" said Diana, "that sounds so interesting. I am eager to begin. You are so kind—"

"I'll see that you get the right books," said the young man looking at his watch with an almost imperceptible movement of his eyes, "and now, if you will excuse me, Ned and I have an engagement and we are overdue already, I believe, so we will have to leave you."

As gracefully as any man she knew he bowed and walked swiftly away, with the boy straight and proud by his side.

"Great work, Pard!" said Neddy under his breath,

"but what I wantta know, Pard, is, why do you monkey with her at all? She's a tough egg, she is. Why, Pard, she can drink more cocktails than all the other girls put together, and smoke more cigarettes, and she has all the fellas on her string, an' keeps each thinking he's the only It. I don't see why you monkey with her at all. She's just tryin' to string you!"

John Dunleith walked along soberly for a moment without speaking. Neddy looked up, almost thinking he had not heard. Then the man looked down at the boy with a smile.

"But she is a living soul, Kid, and my Master cared enough to die for her. There is always a chance that the Bible will reach and do its work."

"Don't kid yourself!" said the worldly wise Neddy.

Diana, standing alone in the flying field, watching them move rapidly down the slope of the hill toward the woods, felt a rising desire to laugh—or cry. When had she ever been dismissed by a young man whom she deigned to honor with her company, in this summary way? It was too vexatious! She simply would not stand such treatment! She would bend him to her power or break him in the attempt. Such insufferable indifference! He had no right to be that way. He pretended to be a gentleman, yet no gentleman she knew would have done what he had done just now, walk off and leave her alone in a field. He should at least have escorted her back to the garden.

She looked up with a start to see Barry standing by her side regarding her almost sternly.

"What have you to do with that fellow?" he asked roughly. "You haven't two ideas in common."

"Really?" she flashed at him, angry at once. "How in the world can you possibly know that?"

"Because he's nothing but a country lout!"

"That's not true!" flashed Diana again, half won-

dering at her own defense of the man whom she had
set out to make the victim of a practical joke. "He's
wearing a Phi Beta Kappa key!"

She did not state that she had just discovered the
key as he swung away to leave her, and that she
knew very little more about the stranger than he
did.

"Well, he's not your kind—not *our* kind—" Barry
added sullenly. "Even if he may be a grind. Come!
Forget him! And for heaven's sake lay off that kind
of thing. Shall we walk or would you rather try
my new car? We could take a drive and bring up
at the country club in time for tea."

"Thanks! I have something else to do!" said Diana
now thoroughly angry, and she flung away and
marched into the house.

For a while she hunted through the library shelves,
and then losing patience she went in search of
Christine and asked the way to Amory's room. She
had remembered that she had seen the new secretary
at church, and of course she would be able to help
her find a Bible.

Amory was surprised on opening her door to find
the golden girl standing there, with almost a friendly
look upon her face.

"Pardon me," said Diana, "could you tell me where
to find a Bible? I want to look up something."

"Why yes," said Amory good-naturedly, handing
out her own which she held in her hand with her
fingers between the leaves. "You may take mine. I
was just through reading anyway."

Diana took it half curiously. It seemed strange to
her that this other girl should be reading a Bible.

"Thanks awfully," she said, "I'll return it in a
little while," and sped away.

Amory went back into her room and sat down with
a hysterical desire to laugh. Her Testament had

sailed away in the air, and now her Bible had gone from her. Was she sent to this house to distribute Bibles to the rich heathen? Now what could that girl want of a Bible? Obviously she had none of her own. Well, it was a puzzle. Perhaps it had something to do with the joke this girl was playing on the minister! She began to wish she had not so easily loaned her Bible. She did not wish to be a party to this outrage, even by so small a contact.

Meanwhile, Diana in a becoming negligee was reclining on a chaise longue, fluttering through the leaves of Amory's well used Bible trying to find the book of Roman's. There did not seem to be any such book in the secretary's Bible, and Diana was beginning to think it must be a different edition from the minister's Bible when she suddenly stumbled upon it. Almost as long it took her to find the chapter. And then when she had read it she closed the book with a puzzled look. What on earth did he mean by giving her a chapter like that to read? What could that possibly have to do with the return of Jesus Christ to the earth?

Puzzling over this question she fell asleep, and was wakened by Christine's tap at her door.

"Please, Miss Dorne, Mr. Dunleith sent these books to you, and he says you'll not need to return them, as he has other copies."

When Christine was gone Diana sat up and examined the package of books curiously. Some of them had queer titles, startling ones, almost as strange as some of the things the minister had said in his sermon. "Our Blessed Hope." Now what could that be? They were most of them small, thin books with inviting print. They did not look at all deep. But they bore on the face of them an atmosphere that was utterly new to her. She never had known there were such books in the world. Why did people bother to write them? Did other people want to know about such things? Did she? Of course she had not really cared to find out but now she felt idly curious to know what it was all about.

At the bottom of the pile she found a little worn Bible with limp black covers, and the name "John Dunleith" and "Edinburgh University" with a recent date below. At that she opened her eyes wider and turned the leaves with deeper interest. Had the young man been to a foreign university? Curious his aunt had not mentioned it. But then he was a silent fellow. Perhaps she did not know it, as she had owned that she had seen very little of him since he was sixteen. Well, that accounted for his general air of culture and refinement.

She felt a curious triumph in finding him out as a student since Barry had tried to discount him. She felt a deeper interest in the young man.

She turned the pages, and found bits of paper marking certain chapters with the references written on the paper, and, idly she glanced them over, but they meant little or nothing to her and she soon threw down the books and began to dress for the evening, this time donning a filmy turquoise chiffon. She resolved more than ever that she would not be balked. She would win that man from his strange reticence. He was probably surrounded by a wall of reserve, and she must find a way to break through and bewitch him. She had never failed before when she had really tried and of course she was not going to fail now. So she threw a string of gleaming crystals over her head and hurried down with a lovely bloom upon her cheeks and an uplifted dreamy look in her turquoise eyes. She had stopped at Amory's door on her way down and left the Bible, and Amory could not help admiring her loveliness. Could she have misjudged her? How lovely she was in that blue frock! It did not seem possible that she could be so false. But why had she wanted the Bible?

Amory had not been called down to tea on the terrace, much to her own relief, for she did not feel in the mood for effacing herself and filling in. Neither, she observed, was the young minister present. Diana held court with Barry and Fred and Clarence, though she cast occasional surreptitious glances toward the garden gate.

Amory's tea was brought to her room, and afterwards she sat till the long shadows outside had lengthened into twilight, having no urge to turn on her lights and read. She would have liked to go to church again, but the long mile and a half through the dark country road with great high hedges on either hand, and only strangers living behind them made her hesitate. Perhaps when she had been here longer and got accustomed to the way in daytime she might venture at night. Or perhaps, sometimes when Christine was off duty she might persuade her to accompany her.

So she sat by her window watching the stars appear one by one, watching the purple mountains fade into velvet darkness, listening to the little sleepy insects, and the tree toads down in the woods, and feeling terribly lonely. Perhaps, too, without knowing it, she was watching for the coming of a plane, listening for the hum of a great motor.

Downstairs the sound of music broke forth, jazz and laughter. How different it all was from home, and the Sunday evenings Aunt Hannah and Aunt Jocelyn loved. Presently while she sat alone and the darkness deepened, with only a luminous hint of the late coming moon over the Eastern mountain, she found the tears flowing softly down, and putting her head down on the arm of the chair she had a good hard cry. It was in the midst of that that Christine tapped at her door and told her someone wanted her on the telephone.

With her heart in her mouth from quick alarm she hurried down the back stairs to the little booth behind the dining room. What had happened at home? Was Aunt Hannah worse? That was surely the only thing that would cause Aunt Jocelyn to waste money on long distance telephoning! Oh, why had she ever come away?

With trembling hand she took up the receiver, and called that frightened "Hello!" then heard that strong young voice greeting her across those hundreds of miles!

And while all this had been going on Diana had been in church! Yes, actually! No, the minister had not taken her. She had initiated the movement herself. After refusing more than once to ride with Barry she told him she would go with him providing he would take her where she wanted to go.

He readily agreed, although she did not tell him their destination until they arrived at the chapel.

Barry was astounded but he acceded, for he knew Diana of old. When she would do something she did it. Into the chapel they went. However, there was more than one way of circumventing a purpose. Barry determined that Diana should have no opportunity to study her preacher during that evening. To that end he exerted himself as only he knew how to do. He sang at the top of his very fine tenor voice, and invented cunning paraphrases of the words that were irresistible. He drew clever caricatures of the minister and the worshipers in the fly leaf of the hymn book. He put his arm around Diana rather openly; he reached for her hand and played with her rings. He talked almost out loud with a running fire of wit that was convulsing. If Diana had been spiritually inclined these things would have been only annoying, as it was they annoyed her neighbors, and merely amused her as Barry had meant they should. Diana had no standards by which to judge herself. She perhaps did not know how utterly obnoxious she was making herself to John Dunleith, nor how completely she was undoing any impression she had intended to make by coming to church.

Diana laughed and whispered a great deal herself, showing her utter indifference to the comfort of those about her so plainly that finally one gray haired woman turned around and looked at her, whereupon the two aliens went off into ill-suppressed mirth that shook the seat and caused others to turn and look at them in scorn.

John Dunleith could not fail to notice all this. Perhaps both Diana and Barry meant that he should. But he went on with his preaching without seeming to look their way until he came to the close. Then he seemed to turn and look straight in their direction. Just one arresting sentence Diana heard, heard and suddenly sobered, a startled look in her eyes. He said, and he seemed to be speaking to her soul:

"You, who were meant to be in the image of God, what will He say to you when you come to stand before the great white throne? Can any one see God in you?"

Barry interposed at this point, calling attention to an old man who had fallen asleep with his mouth open. But Diana did not look at him. She had her eyes on the minister. She was trying to turn over this remarkable question. She did not know why it seemed to pierce her heart like a sudden sword thrust. She did not want to feel what he was saying, but she did. Great white throne! Why should she have to stand before a great white throne? She had never been afraid of anything in her life, but she somehow felt afraid of these words.

"Let's go!" she said suddenly as the sermon closed with a brief prayer, and while the last hymn was being announced they crowded out past three people and left the church. The eyes of the minister as he announced that closing hymn had a sad stern look, but his closing prayer was very tender. When the people crowded around to speak to him afterwards he was as cordial as usual. One of the old elders spoke about the strangers who had made a disturbance, and his eyes grew sad again.

"Yes," said he regretfully, "I'm afraid they don't know the Lord. They need praying for."

"I fear me they're beyond that!" said the sharp old elder spitefully, "I think it would be wasted time."

"Does anybody ever get past the need of prayer?" asked John Dunleith, and went out thoughtfully into the starlight, with Neddy walking proudly by his side.

They came up through the driveway and skirted the house to get to the side entrance, and as they passed the long windows on the terrace a wave of jazz from the radio burst forth straight from some roof garden or cabaret in New York, and Dunleith could see Diana in Barry's close embrace dancing as if her whole soul were in the movement.

She would have been surprised if she had known that John Dunleith went up to his room and knelt to pray for her trifling little soul. Perhaps it would have frightened her if she could have seen into the future.

The moon rose, and the midnight came. The radio was turned off, and the guests at Briarcliffe Manor sought their couches, for there was a heavy day planned for the morrow, and they were all eager to be ready for it. Diana had been one of the first to yawn and say she had had enough of the day and was going to bed. And when Diana was gone somehow the spice of life was wanting, and they all trooped off after her.

The servants went about putting out lights, closing up the castle for the night, and the place grew silent. But still the young preacher knelt in his room and pleaded for the soul of the girl who had plotted to make a fool of him.

And in another part of the house a girl knelt beside a window looking up to the stars, and the clear moonlit sky, and prayed for a man who was sailing somewhere off beneath those stars; and her prayer kept time to the tune of her heart as it sang the one word, "Darling!"

CHAPTER X

THE great bird set sail into a silver sea, and the heart of the flier was at peace. He laughed aloud as he thought what had come to him. The sacred drops on his brow that morning, that had seemed so mysterious when they were put there, so almost useless; the strange words "Child o God I baptize thee in the name of the Father, and o the Son, and of the Holy Ghost," had come to mean something, just with a half hour's explanation. He was born into a new family now. He had become a child of God!

He looked down into the silver sea below him, and saw the world he had left, twinkling little lights like pin points in bunches, those were cities. Great spaces of inky darkness, that was country with the people all gone to bed. Isolated glowing points, those were landmarks, meant for his guidance.

All this wide sea of silver blue was before him, endless lovely spaces through which he must go far before he could come again. The exhilaration of flying was in his veins, the feel of the wheel, his power over his engine, his ability to do this thing he had set out to do, his confidence in himself and his plane, all were a part of the moment as he realized that the race was really on and the world by morning would be standing in wonder watching to see if he could accomplish it.

Yet there was something greater than all this, a feeling of sweet awe, that now, come what might, he was safe. If he met God again out there in the silver-blue he would not be afraid. Whatever happened he was right with God. He might not understand it all, but he believed, and he stood in a new relation to God. Even if he fell, he was in God's hands and all would be well.

Back, in his heart too, nestled a sweet and pleasant thought. A little blue eyed girl, back several hundred miles, was praying for him. Her voice still lingered in his ears, her voice with tears in it, as she promised. He was just as sure she would remember as he was sure he was God's child. She was a stranger only yesterday, but now he stood in a new relationship to her too. She was praying for him as he flew, and he had called her "darling!" He had not meant to, but he was glad he had. Darling! Darling! Darling! What a sweet word that was. Why had he never before noticed what a wonderful word that was?

The night wore on and the sea of crystal in which he sailed was clear as a bell. He never had seen the stars so bright. They seemed like near-by windows into another world. He watched them pale as the dawn drew near, and the sea of silver blue changed into coral and green and gold and orchid, as the sun rose and the day began.

Well on in the morning he was reported to have passed over several towns in Ontario and the papers rushed to set up extra editions and tell the news to the watching world. On and on he rushed, exulting in each mile accomplished. So much nearer the goal, and round to his home again.

Would she be there, waiting? Would she receive him as a friend after this? She would not be angry at that word, "darling," he had called her. Her voice with the tears in it had not sounded angry. She was the one girl in all the world, the girl he had not dreamed there would be anywhere. Oh, if he had known before there was such a girl how different he would have been!

But he was different now. He had been born again! How strange he had been led to that plain little church, to just the thing he had been longing to find out! "Child of God. In the name of the Father, and of the Son, and of the Holy Ghost,"— The drops of water on his brow, like the dew of the morning, he seemed to feel them now, and they were holy, precious!

At noon an observer sighted him as he passed over a small town not far from Fort Nelson. During the afternoon reports came in from several places, showing that he was going steadily on in the course that had been prescribed, though most of them said that while his engine could be heard he was too high up for observation. At eight o'clock in the evening the radio broadcasted the fact that he had just been reported as passing over and signaling Fort Resolution.

The four men in New York sat back in their comfortable chairs with satisfied countenances, and the world held its breath for half a second and listened, exclaiming, and then went on again.

During the night Gareth's engine was heard by prospectors along the Yukon, and early in the morning he climbed the air over the city of Dawson, and dropped a handful of little flags down.

It had been the plan of the sponsors of this flight to have Sitka, Alaska, the first objective, but Gareth had overruled them and chosen Nome as the point where he should refuel and stop for sleep before proceeding to Anadirsk on the coast of Siberia. He wanted to demonstrate the possibility of a non-stop flight between New York and Nome, which no one as yet had tried, and he wanted to cross to Siberia over Bering's Strait, taking the shortest possible course. The Arctic regions lured him, and challenged his courage and prowess. He wanted to do something that nobody else had done.

As he sailed over Dawson he looked down wistfully. He was almost at his first goal, almost ready for the last hard lap of the journey. If he made it as he had planned he would soon be free to go back!

He was climbing over the Canadian Rockies now, snow-capped and mighty in their splendor. The night was clear, and almost like daylight. In fact he was coming into the region of the short Arctic summer night, which meant almost constant daylight, and that was a help of course. He was keeping a steady average now of about one hundred and twelve miles an hour.

But a new foe began to manifest itself, a deadly sleepiness which attacked him from time to time and threatened to overwhelm him. The little closed cabin in which he must ride seemed drugged with drowsiness, the stars seemed waltzing around in the heavens, his eyelids fell shut of themselves, and had to be rubbed open again.

"Now, my Father, help me," he prayed. "Don't let this get me!" and again he found himself repeating "Name of the Father, and of the Son, and of the Holy Ghost!"

It was deadly, this sleep that was coming over him, like a featherbed that enveloped him, and choked out all sense. Even the gleaming mountain peaks had faded from his vision. He might run into one and not know it until it was too late. He must do something about this.

He moved himself about as much as he could and tried to stir up a circulation; he adjusted his ventilators so that there was more air.

Presently he began to notice something queer about his compass. It was not working right—or was his own brain muddled with this deadly sleep? It seemed that his course had veered from the straight line his instinct taught him was right. Sometimes the nearness of the North Pole did play havoc with a compass needle. But still, if he could not trust his compass what else was there to do? He certainly could not guide himself through these unknown wastes of air.

So he held on his way, hour after hour, pinching himself to keep awake, inventing all sorts of tortures to keep the great torture from drawing him into its deadly alluring arms.

And now by his watch the morning was well on its way, the second morning of his trip, and soon he ought to be nearing Nome. Had he crossed the Yukon River yet? He peered down but he could not tell. The whole world seemed one mass of white peaks, or was that water far below?

It was his eyes of course that were full of sleep. His eyes that saw fields of snow rolling like billows. Just his eyes, blinded by the long strain, and the whiteness, and the sunlight. Or was that really water he was over—a wide sea! A horror froze in his throat. Had he missed his way? Was his compass really wrong? And was this Alaska Bay he was crossing, or had he come too far North and was this the Arctic Sea?

By his mileage now he ought to be at Nome, but there was no sign of human habitation. A glance at his compass showed it acting queerly, jumping around like a human thing that had lost its mind. Ah! This deadly cold and this smothering sleep! Why had he ever tried to do this fool thing?

It was about that time that he suddenly noticed a fine gray mist on his windshield. Was he coming into a storm? No, the barometer showed no change in weather conditions! Yet he could not see now where he was going. He looked about and the fine gray mist was all over on every side, the world outside being gradually obliterated. Was he going blind? He must be cool about this. He must not get excited. Even a blind man might be able to do something about it. There was his wireless, too, and now he noticed he could still see everything inside his cabin with perfectly clear vision. Ah! The trouble was outside. He opened his windshield a little way and the bitter cold rushed in, and the clear bright light of day, and suddenly he knew what was the matter. His oil line had broken! That spelled disaster!

Was the oil going fast? Could he keep his plane in the air until he was over a safe landing? It would be a risk of course, for if the oil was gone the engine would stop.

He peered out through the open windshield, but there was nothing below him but that wide heaving blue sea with the white white mountains floating in it! Were they islands or icebergs? If he only knew where he was!

And now he saw as he looked outside how everything was covered with that gray sooty oil, thick and black on the windows. There was no hope that he could stay up in the air until he reached Nome, or —somewhere. His ship was doomed. His engine had stalled. He must come down, and come down mighty soon! But where?

Again he looked below him. There was nothing but that endless rolling blue-white sea, and the jagged towering icebergs, sailing like complacent ships, slowly, so slowly, they seemed but restless mountains of crystal, just come alive a little. There was a space on the great one just before him, that looked like a level spot. Yet he knew that icebergs were treacherous things. He knew they had wide crevasses, and soft spots in them where they were about to part asunder. An iceberg was no kind of a place to land! Yet there was no other but the sea.

Slowly, cautiously, he dropped his plane, keeping to the end that cool courage for which many a newspaper in the triumphal days past had commended him.

Like a sick bird the great ship dropped, the master keeping control in a graceful glide. He suddenly felt so small, and his plane with its mighty engine so helpless, there above that wide heaving sea of sparkling ice.

It was happening to him, then, just as it had happened to hundreds of others! This was how they all had felt! He had come to the end and there was no hope for him on this earth!

The papers to-morrow morning would say he was lost at sea! They would send out a few planes to search for him, but his body would be beneath those icy waters, or wrecked on one of those jagged peaks! Then they would come back, and the papers would tell all his feats, and all the flags would be at half mast for a few days, and he would be forgotten. But they would not tell how he was a child of God, and had been saved and would live forever. They did not know he was going to live forever with God!

But God was here, and he was the child of God now.

"Oh, God!" he spoke aloud, with his hand firmly on the controls of the machine and his eyes straight ahead as he swooped low over the white forbidding field, just as if God were down there waiting for him, showing him where to guide his machine, "God, I am your child, and I'm trusting you!"

Would the little girl remember after the others had forgotten? Would they find the little book floating on the water perhaps and send it back to her? Would she know? He was glad he had called her darling! It would not matter now, and she would not mind after this. Oh, death made a great difference in things!

He must be almost down now. Yes— Ah! A grinding! Steady— Steady! He must not lose control. If this was an iceberg it would be rough. There might be sharp walls ahead of his ship! There—! "God! Are you there?"

The light went out with a crash, and he lay in darkness and pain, and then even that was obliterated.

"God! Child of God! Name of the Father, Name of the Son—"

CHAPTER XI

EXCITEMENT in the Whitney mansion ran high Monday morning when the morning paper was read. Ned rushed to turn on the radio at once to make sure he did not miss an announcement concerning his other cousin who was also a hero in his eyes, though not quite so companionable a pal heretofore as Cousin John.

"It's fool nonsense!" said the master of the house attacking his grapefruit fiercely. "What's it all for anyway? Just so that some corporation or other can carry gold from Nome to New York in a few hours. Well, what's Siberia got to do with it all?"

"Probably they expect us all to migrate there and settle," suggested Fred who always had some solution of any question propounded.

"I certainly would like to have gone with him!" said Diana wistfully, watching under the fringes of her lashes to see if John Dunleith heard her.

"I expect that's why he went off without telling us," said Caroline discontentedly. "He never did want girls along when he was doing anything interesting."

"Who would want a girl along on a trip like that?" said Mr. Whitney. "In my opinion a woman who goes on a trip like that demeans herself. She simply does it to get before the eyes of the world, and if she gets wrecked she deserves all she gets!"

"Oh, mercy! Daddy! How mid-Victorian!" cried Caroline.

"I was just thinking of buying a plane myself and taking up flying," said Diana sweetly, archly, looking at her host.

"I still think so!" declared the host without smiling, whereat they all shrieked together.

Amory, summoned to the dining room to do an errand for Mrs. Whitney, turned away and looked out of the window. It seemed a desecration to hear them carrying on this way when one who was recently of their number was sailing the skies alone.

The paper lay on the floor and as she stood there ostensibly waiting for Mrs. Whitney to write out a list of the people she wanted called on the telephone, she could read it from where she stood. In great letters across the page she saw:

TED KINGSLEY FLIES TO SIBERIA

**Hopping off at midnight, the cheerful pilot
Makes Ontario before daybreak!**

She read it with an inward shudder. Somehow it seemed so tragic to have them talk of it in this light way, as if he were playing a few holes of golf, or trying to win a set of tennis.

He did not seem the same person as the Gareth who had bade her good-by last night over the telephone.

As quickly as she could she got away from the giddy company, and from that dreadful newspaper; though later in the day when she had opportunity she walked down to the village and brought up all the papers she could find. It seemed she must know every word they said about him even though it made her unhappy to read them.

After she had read them all she put them away

carefully out of sight. No one must suspect that she had any interest in the young man!

But later, Christine came up on an errand and gave the latest news about the flyer which had come in on the radio, and after she had gone Amory went to the window and looked out and far, as if she by straining her eyes could see to that far sky line where he flew, the man who had dared to call her darling! And ever she kept praying in her heart for his safety.

The young people had gone for a horseback ride. Horses had been brought up from the riding club, smart riding togs had been donned, and the party had mounted and ridden away. Diana had looked adorable in a brilliant scarlet coat and little shiny red boots, a red cap crowning her shining hair. Diana could wear any color and look better in it than any one else.

Amory watched them ride away, standing at her window. She was getting a regular habit of standing there, watching and living in other people's lives. It was like reading a fairy tale.

Mr. Whitney watched them ride away, also, standing down on the terrace with his wife, and his voice was quite distinct as he spoke in a startled voice:

"Why, where is John? Why isn't he with them? I ordered horses enough. Did no one call him?"

"Oh, Sam Marsden came over. They had to ask him to go of course. Besides, John wouldn't want to go. He never has anything to do with the rest. They are not at all congenial, you know," answered his wife.

"Why aren't they congenial, I'd like to know?" asked the master of the castle raising his voice, angrily. "Isn't my nephew good enough for them? They're a nice bunch I'll say! Camp down in my house, and eat my food, and ride the horses I pay for, and then snub my nephew! I'll—!"

"Hush, Henry! They'll hear you!" warned his wife.

"Let them hear me!" he shouted raising his voice a little louder. "If they don't hear me now they will when they come back. I'll let them know what I think of a bunch that will romp all over my house, and order my servants around, and smoke my cigarettes, and get under foot everywhere, and then treat my nephew as if he was the dust under their feet!"

"Hush, Henry! Don't you know that John will hear you. You don't want to hurt his feelings do you."

"Hurt his feelings! *I* hurt his feelings? How would I hurt his feelings when I'm taking his part?"

"Why you are letting him know that you suspect them of being impolite to him. He will think that you think he is not good enough—"

"Nothing of the kind! What do you take him for? Don't you suppose he knows already how those young dudes and simpering fools that call themselves women are acting toward him? Don't you suppose he has eyes in his head? Did *you* think he was a fool, too? Well, he's not, and I'll tell you another thing. He's got the number of every one of these wild idiots your daughters have gathered around them, and there isn't one of them that is worth John's little finger so far as brains and good sense are concerned. Wouldn't be congenial, I should say not—not to *him!*"

"Well, then, Henry dear—" said his wife soothingly, "why do you make such a fuss about it? If John wouldn't enjoy them why should you want to force them on him? Why not let him have pleasure in his own way?"

"Because, John is my nephew and I'm not going to have him insulted in my house!" said the master hotly. "Because John is a gentleman, and he is not going to show his preferences the way these young hyenas you have here do! He came here expecting to make himself agreeable, even if he had to go a few places he didn't want to go, and be entertaining to a few people who weren't in his mental class at all; and by all that's decent he's going to have a chance to show them how much better he is than they are, or they're all going to get out before night. See? I'm about sick of this mess anyway, silly little fools of girls all dolled up with their spinal column showing, and their knees bare, making eyes at me and being impudent in the same breath, and turning my daughters into selfish little beasts like themselves!"

"Henry! The servants will hear you!"

"Let them hear! They have found it out long ago. They'll see that I have as much discernment as they have. You don't suppose the servants don't see the weaknesses of the people they serve?"

"They have no right to criticise their betters!" said Mrs. Whitney with dignity. "If I thought one of them dared even *think* a criticism of us and our guests I would dismiss them at once."

"Oh, you would, would you? Well, you wouldn't show any better sense than the kids then. Why haven't they a right to criticise, I'd like to know? You don't pay them to give up thinking do you? Isn't this a free country? And when it comes right down to that the only girl in this house that has a modest quiet decent way with her is that pretty little secretary you've just imported. If you ask me, now, there's a girl I'd like to have my daughters associate with. There's a girl that can dress up sweetly, and look like a flower, and carry herself well; and she doesn't sprawl all over the place trying to exhibit her clothes and herself, and trying to say something smart. She doesn't try to get every fool boy on her string, nor plot to make a stranger fall in love with her."

Amory at her window suddenly sat down in her chair and buried her face in her two hands, the color flooding her cheeks. Oh, she never plotted to make a strange man fall in love with her, but what would Mr. Whitney think if he knew who had called her on the telephone at eleven o'clock Sunday night? What would he think if he ever found those two little silver wings now hidden away in the depths of her trunk?

But the voice outside stormed on.

"The young men nowadays are most of them fools, anyway, or worse. John is the only one that is a real man, with the possible exception of your nephew Ted, and I think he's wasting his life, flying around in the sky when he ought to get his feet down on earth and do something really worth while. However, he *thinks* he's doing something that amounts to something, and that's more than the others do. He's got his nerve with him, I'll hand him that. But these others, Bah! They make me sick! They have only nerve to be insolent, and effeminate! Take that Blaine fellow. Why, he's a drunk! That's all there is to him! Why you are willing to have him around with your daughters—I can't understand! Of course he isn't paying much attention to them I'll grant, not even enough to be polite while he's in their father's house, but I wouldn't want them even to *see* a specimen like that! I wouldn't want their standards lowered to that extent. But perhaps you think that they never had any standards to lower, and I guess you're right!"

"Henry!" tearfully, "you are disgracing us!"

"Is that possible? I thought we had already fallen too low to be disgraced! What is it they call it when a quantity of water gets as much of a solution as it can assimilate, a saturate solution? Well, I thought we had about reached that stage. I thought we had a saturate solution of disgrace in our family. After that affair Caroline had with that poor fool in Florida last winter, and the night we found Doris out with Standish Mortimer at three—!"

"Henry! Stop! I shall not listen to another word!" sobbed Mrs. Whitney, turning to go into the house.

"Here! No, you're not going to get out of it that way, Leila! You can come right back here and listen till I'm through. I've just one more thing to say, and I'm going to say it and you're going to hear it if I have to raise my voice still higher. I want it understood that John is to go on everything that goes on here while this infernal party lasts. If he doesn't I'll take pleasure in sending all these ill-mannered guests to their homes with a few frank parting words. Now, do you understand?"

"Why certainly, Henry! Of course we will ask him if you wish!" said the tearful, self-controlled voice of Mrs. Whitney, looking anxiously toward the upper windows to see if any one was listening, "I should have attended to it long before if I had understood that it was your wish. I supposed of course that you would want John to feel at home here and do just as he pleased, and I am sure he has had all freedom—"

"He certainly has!" said his uncle vindictively. "The only member of the family who has even lifted an eyelash toward him since his arrival is our son who has utterly monopolized him, which only goes to prove that John is entirely unselfish. Now—from now on things change! Take that parade to the Old Fort that is being pulled off to-morrow—utterly ridiculous of course, because no one wants to see the ramshackle place, but you've started it so it must go through—take along a big lunch and eat with bugs running around in your mouth and ants on your fingers, and sit on the ground with your legs curled in uncomfortable positions—however, you're going! And *John is going too!*"

"But I'm not sure he'll want to go, Henry!"

"I'll see that he goes anyway!"

"But Henry—"

"No, 'But-Henrys!' He's going or nobody goes! Not one of our cars will go that trip unless John is invited by you and by Caroline and Doris to go also. What's more it's got to be a cordial invitation too, and given at the dinner table where I can hear it and where everybody else can hear it! And if it isn't just as well done as you would do it for that sneak of a Barry Blaine who snoops around and tries to find my wine closet when no one is looking, I'll just can the whole show. That's final! You can do as you please, but you know what to expect if you do."

With which parting shot the gentleman of the house retired to his den, while his wife, breathless, and tearful, with a bright red spot on each cheek which was not put there artificially, beat a hasty retreat to her room to repair damages before any one saw her.

So John Dunleith went along the next day on the drive.

Whether he wanted to go along or not is another story. But two things had conspired to make him willing, and he went. The first reason was that his uncle had dropped a word just before dinner that evening.

"John, I suppose it will bore you to death to go on that jamboree with the bunch to-morrow, but I'd be awfully obliged if you felt you could. I don't like to have the kid go without some one along to look after him, and the rest are all too busy with their own affairs. And then, too, I don't feel any too certain of that Blaine fellow. He drinks like a fish, and you never know what he's up to. If you can just manage to keep an eye on his operations I'll be doubly thankful."

Of course John felt that he must go, though he knew of almost nothing he would not rather do.

The other reason was Blaine himself. Dunleith had been watching how things were going, and for some reason he could not bring himself to forget the girl for whom he had been praying. That she was a frivolous worldly creature, treacherous and untrue with all her beauty, he did not doubt, yet something in her appealed to him for protection. He might be a fool, he probably was, but he decided to go along.

A much surprised boy was Neddy when he was informed by his father that he was to go along. He opened his mouth to protest loudly. He hated the crowd, and he knew they hated him. It bored him to death to take a long drive with older people and he had plans of his own.

But the father added that Cousin John was going also, and Neddy broke forth with a whoop of joy.

Mrs. Whitney gave the compulsory invitation most gracefully at dinner, though her daughters almost spoiled it all with their expressions of dismay.

"Great Cats! What has come over Mamma Whitney?" whispered Susanne to Caroline as they rose from the dinner table. "Why does she want to stick us all day with that poor fish? He doesn't speak two words to any of us."

"It's not Mamma, it's Daddy," declared the wise

daughter. "He's probably made a point of it, and when Dad makes a point of a thing Mother is wise enough to agree with him. But he won't bother us. They're sending the kid, too, and they'll probably go off somewhere together."

"Well, for heaven's sake, don't put him in the car with me. I had my dose of him the night I took him at the table just to show Diana. I thought I'd pass out. We haven't two ideas in common!"

Diana did not show by so much as the turn of an eyelash that she had heard the minister invited, but later, when they had all gone into the library to turn on the radio and see if there was news of the flier, she slipped up behind him and said in a low tone:

"Mr. Dunleith, I'm very glad you're to go with us to-morrow, for I want very much to have you tell me what all those books you sent me mean. You'll think I'm very stupid perhaps, but I just couldn't get head nor tail of any of them."

"Perhaps you began at the wrong end," said the young man, smiling enigmatically.

"What do you mean?"

"I mean that to the natural man these things are foolishness. Spiritual things must be spiritually discerned."

"Well," said Diana, "how do you do that? Can't you tell me to-morrow?"

"If you are in earnest."

"Yes, I'm in earnest," said the girl lifting clear liquid eyes to his face, eyes that would deceive the very elect with their loveliness. But what she saw in his eyes was utter doubt of her, and in spite of her nonchalance she colored.

"You don't think I am!" she challenged.

"No, I don't think you are," said the young man

with a drawing of breath that sounded like a sigh.

"You have no right to say that!" said Diana in a vexed tone.

"Haven't I?" he asked, looking searchingly into her face.

"I'm sure I don't know what you mean," she said again, half angry, but the more determined to get him to tell her. "I want to understand you very much. I want to know what it is that makes you different."

"Different?"

"Yes, you are different. I can't understand it. You are good looking and well educated, you are young, can talk well and act well, and could be popular if you half tried, and you don't seem to get a thing out of life for yourself."

He smiled.

"I suppose I ought to thank you for painting such a pleasant portrait of me, but you see the truth is I've found something better than just getting things out of life for myself."

"What is it?" she asked eagerly, and there was a ring of genuineness to her tone for the first time.

He studied her a moment and then he said earnestly:

"It is to let God get the best He has planned for me out of life."

"Oh!" she said, her face perceptibly lengthened, "but why? How? I'm sure I don't understand at all what you mean? It seems such a perfect waste, you young and good looking, and bright, and able to do something worth while in the world, to be shut up to a stuffy thing like preaching to a lot of old women and children. What's the good of it all, anyway? I wish you'd give it all up and get into some real business, and be my friend. I like you, see? It makes me cross to have you waste your splendid self on such things when we might have such good times if you only would be reasonable. Come, here's a challenge! Be a good sport and a real man! I can't bear to think of you wasted this way."

"You mean," said the young man looking at her amusedly, "you mean that you want me to play around with you for a little while and have a good time. You don't care in the least whether my life is wasted or not. You just want to see me do as the other men do that you like. Come, be honest and own up!"

She turned from him with offended air:

"Oh, well, of course, if you are going to continue to doubt me," she said and made a move as if to leave him.

"I wish with all my soul I did not have to," he said sadly. "I wish that you were as beautiful as you look. I wish that you really wanted to know what has come into my life that has made me different from what I used to be."

"Well, I do," said Diana suddenly with a desire born of the moment showing keenly in her eyes. "Tell me! There is something and it is real. Tell me now. I want to understand it. I think you have no right to treat me this way."

"Perhaps not," said John Dunleith, still studying her face. "Well then, come outside and we will walk a few minutes and I will tell you."

So, much to the disappointment of Neddy who was hovering outside the long window hoping that Cousin John would come and tell him more about the stars, and how airplanes were made, as he did last night, John Dunleith stepped out into the moonlight with Diana by his side.

He did not ask her to take his arm, and Diana for some strange reason, perhaps fearing to break the charm of her brief success, did not dare.

When they had walked quite away from the house he spoke:

"It is very simple," he said, "yet I am not sure you will understand. It is something you have got to experience yourself before you can know what it means. And there is always self standing in the way of personal experience."

"Go on, please," she urged.

"Well, five years ago I came to know myself as a sinner, and Jesus Christ as my Saviour."

"A sinner? *You?*" said the girl in astonishment.

"Yes, a sinner. Some day you will know yourself that way."

Diana visibly shrank and was silent.

"Since then," went on the steady voice, "it is my greatest joy to let others know of the salvation that has come to me. Besides, you know, He's coming back!"

"There! That's it!" cried Diana suddenly arresting his voice, "that's what I don't understand. What on earth do you mean by that? You don't really believe that the One they call Jesus is coming back to the earth again, after He died all those years ago?"

"I certainly do."

"Why do you think that?"

"Because He said He would."

"You mean He said so when He was alive? You mean the Bible tells about it?"

"Yes."

"But why do you think He knew about the future any more than any other man that ever lived?"

"Because He was God!"

Diana shivered.

"When is He coming?" she asked sharply. "When do you think He is coming?"

"We do not know that. We are told that we must watch for it, and that those who do so will have great blessing, but that the day and hour of His coming is known only to God, the Father, not even to the angels in heaven. But there are signs of His coming. And by those we know that He must be coming now very soon."

"Signs? What signs?"

There was a frightened look in the girl's eyes as she watched his face.

"Oh, signs of the times to-day, the Jews establishing their nation at Jerusalem for one thing—"

"Diana! Oh, Diana! Where are you? We're coming out to dance on the lawn by moonlight!" called Susanne, and a bevy of young people detached themselves from the house and came toward the two who were walking down by the garden.

"Will you tell me more about this to-morrow?" asked Diana putting a detaining hand upon his arm as she saw him about to stand aloof.

"Yes, if there is opportunity," he answered gravely, and then saw her whirled away by Barry to the tune of a blaring radio.

A few minutes later Amory was not surprised to be summoned to Mrs. Whitney's rooms, and told that her presence would be required on the excursion the next day. She would have to look after the serving of the lunch which would be packed in hampers and taken along.

Amory knew that Mrs. Whitney had come on the terrace a few minutes before, and had seen Diana and John Dunleith walking together in the garden. The inference was obvious. Mrs. Whitney for some reason was trying to prevent Diana from any designs upon the young minister, and Amory could not believe that it was for the minister's sake. Was she, perhaps reserving Diana for her nephew, Theodore Kingsley? The thought was somehow not pleasant to her.

CHAPTER XII

THE party started off very early in the morning, early, that is for them. It was a matter of nine o'clock or a little after. They ate their breakfast in a wild gale of laughter and jokes, and in the midst of it all the radio crisped in with a message about the flier. He had passed Fort Resolution between eight and nine o'clock the night before, and should be well on his way to Nome.

They paused long enough to hear and then broke forth into hilarious excitement again.

Amory, going about with Christine gathering up the different portions of the bountiful lunch, and stowing them in hampers, felt that her heart was not in her work. Oh! that she might remain at the house and work hard, rather than go with this joyous crowd who didn't care that their friend was in the air, after such a long strain. Sometimes she wondered at herself for caring so much for this stranger and then she would remember his good-by—"Darling!" and the color would spring to her cheeks and the light to her eyes. Who would ever have imagined that she would turn out romantic just like all silly girls! So she chided herself, and worked gravely, carefully.

Mrs. Whitney had arranged the young people in the cars at least so far as it affected John Dunleith, Neddy and her secretary. She put them all in one of the servants' small cars with a chauffeur to drive, but she paid well for it afterwards. For the master of the house discovered what she had done as that last car rounded the curve from the garage and drove away.

"What on earth is John doing in that car with Christine and the chauffeur? Why isn't he in with the other young people?" he demanded furiously.

"I'm sure I don't see why you act that way, Henry," soothed his wife. "You surely know that the young people pile in as they wish and it would be hard to restrain them. I think John is very well satisfied. He said he didn't in the least mind Richard and Christine riding with them. He has the lovely girl with him that you admired so extravagantly yesterday, and I have an idea they won't worry much about the rest. Of course Neddy is there as one of the family. John shouldn't be hurt."

But Henry Whitney fumed and stormed, and declared that this was the last house party he would countenance; until his wife was glad to escape to her room and rest for a while. It was a part of the plan that the host and hostess should drive up to the Old Fort a couple of hours later, and be there to take lunch with the young people. By that time Henry would be smoothed down, and have forgotten. And anyway Leila Whitney was glad she had kept Diana from riding with John. Such a ridiculous pairing off as that was, and that silly joke that might bring trouble later if she did not stop it! Of course Henry must not be allowed to know her reasons, but she felt she had acted most wisely. When Teddy came back all would be well. Teddy knew how to manage Diana, and Teddy was crazy about her. Such a lovely wife Diana would make for Teddy. Just a charming couple. Leila Whitney was a born match maker. Besides, she had an eye to Barry for Caroline. Caroline had always been fond of him, though he never would look at her when Diana was about. Of course Barry was a little wild, and Henry had the most unreasoning dislike for him, but Barry would settle down. There was nothing like a nice wife to settle a man down. So she reasoned as she submitted herself to the hands of her maid for a facial, and a shampoo, and then a rest before it was time to go. Poor Teddy! She did hope he would soon be somewhere that he could rest a little! This flying really was awfully hard on one's family. She felt exhausted just knowing that he had been flying on all these hours without sleep!

Then she dropped off into a nice doze and forgot all about her dead brother's only child far away in the icy air.

John Dunleith and Neddy and Amory had a pleasant ride in the back seat, with Christine in front with the chauffeur. The conversation naturally was brought down to Neddy's level, and it was surprising how many things along the roadside were made to serve as topics of interest. There were peculiar flowers growing like broidery in a field, and the minister knew all about their formation and habits. He knew their botanical names, and a lot of interesting things about them. He also knew when a song sparrow was singing and when it was a meadow lark they heard; knew the flash of a cardinal's wing, and what the blue birds did in winter. He could tell a snake story of the far west that made their hair stand on end, or he could describe a base ball game till they almost saw the first batter slide to base. He knew some of the big league players, had been to college with them, and told amusing anecdotes about them. And once when they were passing a peculiarly beautiful view he said it reminded him of a symphony, and he began to describe the music until even Neddy was interested, and sat dreamily watching the landscape and seeing things he had never noticed before. It had never occurred to him that beautiful mountains and trees meant anything. He had always taken them for granted.

Amory asked a few questions, by and by, about the Sunday sermon, and Neddy listened as if he understood and was interested, especially when the conversation turned on the recent troubles between the Jews and Arabs in Jerusalem, and Dunleith told of his travels in that land.

Then they spoke of the flier. The minister, it appeared, had been in Siberia during the war. And the talk drifted to the far lands, with many a thrill, till even Christine and the chauffeur were openly listening.

On the whole, that entire car full were sorry when they reached the old Fort and the party had to get out and begin to try to have a good time.

They walked about a while, looking at the old building, and reading various inscriptions. Then for ten cents they went through a building that professed to be a museum and looked at various relics of an old war long forgotten, and the company broke up into groups again.

Coming out into the bright world once more from the stuffy museum everybody decided it was time to have lunch, so Amory and Christine with the help of Dunleith and the chauffeur began to get the hampers out. Dunleith discovered as he passed Barry Blaine that he had already visited the hamper of bottles that seemed to be an inevitable accompaniment of any festivity with this group. Barry was noisy and dictatorial. He insisted that Diana go off with him into the woods to hunt wild flowers.

The elder Whitneys arrived about the time that
the lunch was set forth, and the young people gathered back like a swarm of hungry bees to honey.

The meal was hilarious, and the liquor flowed
freely. Amory in her capacity of assistant had opportunity to see how often some of the young men,
especially Barry, visited the hamper where the bottles lay.

John Dunleith proved himself a most efficient
helper. He looked after every one's comfort, and did
little unobtrusive things like discovering that some
one was without olives, or needed another sandwich,
and supplying the need. Neither was he a silent
automaton. As if the crowd had been a congenial
one, just as if they were a group of college fellows
he knew well, he entered as far as he could into the
mirth of the hour, saying witty things, giving bright
answers, and making them all look at him in surprise. Some of the girls quite warmed to his favor,
and considered whether after all he might not be
worth cultivating.

But as soon as the lunch things were cleared away,
Dunleith and Neddy disappeared from the scene into
the woods, so they had no further opportunity to
cultivate him.

Amory had wandered off by herself to sit down
under a tree when she saw that all the work was
done. She had no desire to sit on the edge of a group
and try to pretend she was one of the girls. She knew
they did not want her, and she certainly did not
want them under those conditions. So she sat and
looked at the sky, which was beginning now to cloud
over. She wondered if it were clear up in Alaska,
and whether there would be news of the flier when
they reached home. She reflected that if they had
only seen fit to leave her at home she might have had

a nice time reading in the library, and perhaps venturing to turn on the radio to see if there were further information about the flight.

She took out a book she had brought with her to read, but glancing back to the spot where they had eaten lunch she saw Christine standing alone, looking rather forlorn. The chauffeur had strolled away with his pipe. Evidently he and Christine had nothing in common either.

An idea came to her, and she turned it over in her mind for a moment or two before she acted upon it. Why shouldn't she be nice to Christine? Of course she would be practically classing herself with a servant, but what matter? She had no part with these other girls. She had no class to lose. It could hurt nobody but herself, and that only in the eyes of the young people who thought nothing of her anyway. So she got up and went over to Christine.

"Come over here and let us read this story together," she said pleasantly. "I'm sure you're bored having to stand around all alone, and so am I."

"Oh, thank you, Miss Lorrimer," said Christine gratefully, "but you mustn't put yourself out for me. I'll do very well. I'm used to it."

"Well, come, I'd like it," smiled Amory pleasantly, and Christine came. So they sat together under the big tree with a wide valley spread out before them, and a purple mountain or two in the distance, and read their story. Presently they were just two girls laughing together over a funny situation of the heroine, and smiling in sympathy when the crisis turned and brought the hero to his desired goal.

"See those two!" said Mr. Whitney, standing by his wife as they started out to walk about the hillside. "What did I tell you! That secretary is a real girl! There's no snobbery about her. You never had one before that didn't order the maids around as if she were paying them."

"Oh, really, Henry, you are quite impossible!" sighed his wife. "Don't you know that that only shows she is quite common? No self-respecting secretary would mingle with the help. They would know it was lowering to their station. But she doesn't seem even to know. I suppose she is no better than Christine, though she was very highly recommended."

"Christine is all well enough in her place, and better than most maids you've had, but this little Lorrimer girl is a gem. She's intelligent too. I caught her reading some very deep books in the library. It's all wrong this class business, anyway. Why isn't one girl as good as another?"

"Well, you talk a great deal!" snapped his wife, "but I haven't noticed you hobnobbing with the chauffeur. And you seem to enjoy being waited upon as much as I do. Besides, you wouldn't want Caroline and Doris to be intimate with Christine, you know you wouldn't."

"Fat chance I'd have of getting them to do it, if I did want it," snapped the father. "Caroline and Doris are queens of all the snobs I know. Perhaps I wouldn't want them to spend their time playing tennis with Christine, because she's earning her living working for you, but I certainly would like to see them show a little human kindess to another girl who lives under the same roof with them. This morning I heard Caroline giving Christine a terrible going over for not picking up some garment she had left on the floor, and it was the most unkind line of words I've ever been witness to. It's time you spoke to those two daughters of yours about treating the servants a little more decently."

"How about you doing it. They are your daughters too, aren't they?"

They wrangled on, looking with unseeing eyes at a marvelous panorama of valley and hill and mountain, and finally wandered into the woods to hunt up the various groups of young people and see how things were going.

Down in the woods there was a stream, still and beautiful, under trailing hemlocks, and there were canoes that could be hired. Most of the young people had divided into groups and were off in canoes. John Dunleith and Neddy had been up stream as far as it was navigable down again to the falls, and now were coming up once more, Neddy had persuaded John to let him paddle stern, and John was paddling at the bow with swift silent strokes that hardly made a ripple in the smooth surface, nor disturbed the little water bugs that were waltzing on its sheen. As they rounded a great moss-covered rock that bulged out into the water, they heard voices just above them on the bank angry voices, and the sound of a brief struggle. Then swift feet running down the hillside, stepping on the little crackling twigs, and starting small stones rolling down to the water. A moment more, and they came where they could see her.

It was Diana, looking like a dryad, dressed in leaf brown, a little brown cap on her gold hair. She looked angry and excited and had apparently not expected any one along just then. She was twisting her white fingers and walking restlessly along the bank, coming toward them.

"Steer up to the bank, Pal, and take her in. She needs us, don't you see?"

Neddy obediently turned toward the mossy rock between the girl and the canoe.

"Won't you ride with us, Miss Dorne?" asked

Dunleith pleasantly. "It's much nicer than walking."

Diana stopped and a smile bloomed out on her lips.

"I'd love to," she said, with a furtive glance back and up the hill.

"Hang on to that tree trunk, Pal, and hold the canoe steady there. Now, Miss Dorne, if you will give me your hand, and just step down to this seat, so. Are you comfortable? Want a cushion? Heave that cushion back here, Neddy boy! Now, are we all set? Let's go!"

Diana leaned back on the back rest, and drew a breath of relief.

"This is nice!" she said looking up at the arching trees that nearly met overhead. "I'm fed up with this picnic. I hate picnics anyway, don't you? I ran away from—them—all!" she added with another furtive glance back and up the hill.

They drifted on down to the falls a little way, and turned up stream again, and when they returned to the rock where Diana had embarked there stood Barry, uncertainly, balanced on the slippery moss, frowning, and blinking at her in wonder.

Diana flung him one defiant glance and turned her back on him, and in a moment they were gone on around the great rock and out of sight, with strong quick silent strokes of the paddles, so that she breathed freely again.

They did not talk much. Now and again John Dunleith would call attention to some bird, or lovely creeping vine covered with bright red berries. He stopped and gathered one for Diana, carefully, not to break off the berries, taking it up by the roots, and she swathed it as carefully in her handkerchief. She seemed like a new little girl now, just having a good time, and not at all like the Diana of the house party who was flirting with every man, and wending her imperious way wherever she liked.

They went up as far as they could, to where little rapids rippled over mossy stones, and a row of stepping stones crossed the stream. They lingered in a little bay or notch beneath a group of dripping hemlocks that hung their fronds down to the water.

"It is lovely here," said Diana. "I would like to stay here. How it rests one. I'm awfully tired of things, aren't you?"

"Why no!" said John with a smile, "I think life is interesting But I like this too. I could enjoy staying here awhile."

"I wish you would tell me something," said Diana after a pause during which she had broken off several small twigs of hemlock to sniff their fragrance.

"Gladly if I can," said the young man, shipping his paddle carefully lest it should drip on the passenger.

"Well, I wish you'd tell me why you sent me that queer chapter in the Bible to read! It didn't have a thing to do with what you had been talking about in church and it certainly didn't seem to have a thing to do with me. It sounded as if it were meant for some one being tried in a court of justice."

John Dunleith smiled.

"That was the sixth chapter of Romans, wasn't it? So you thought that had nothing to do with you? But you're mistaken. It has to do with every person on this earth."

"But how?"

"Didn't you know we were all sinners?"

"Are you calling me a sinner?" asked Diana, sitting up stiffly, and speaking with a crisp offense in her voice.

"I didn't call you a sinner. God called us sinners because we have all broken His law."

"I'm not a sinner!" said Diana offended. "You may call me that if you like, but I don't feel that I'm a sinner!"

"Perhaps that was just the reason I gave you that chapter to read. I wanted you to learn that you are a sinner, because until you understand that, there is no hope for you. But the very last verse gives you hope, right along with the condemnation. 'The wages of sin is death,—but the gift of God is eternal life through Jesus Christ our Lord.' Read farther and see what it says. 'There is therefore now no condemnation to them that are in Christ Jesus.'"

Suddenly into the midst of his words there came a thundering sound of automobile horns, three or four of them tooting together. It was the sound that had been agreed upon to call the party together when they were to leave, and it came with startling, almost insulting clearness, breaking into their talk.

"I don't want to go back," said Diana pouting, "I want to stay here and talk. Let's don't go back. Let's stay here till they've gone. They'll leave a car for us. They didn't intend to leave before seven, and it's only six."

"I'm afraid that wouldn't be quite square," said the minister, his paddle already in position for action. "There may be some reason for their going so soon. We'd better answer the call. Then if they are willing to leave a car we can come back."

He lifted his face suddenly and looked above.

"Ah!" he said sharply, "there's the reason! Look how black the sky is getting! There is going to be a big storm. We shall have to hurry to make it before the rain comes."

"Oh, what a pest!" said Diana looking up at the black sky. "I was having the first nice time today."

Dunleith gave her one of those penetrating

glances, that seemed to pierce beneath the surface, and wrench the truth right out of her heart.

"I was!" she assured him smiling. "I never had such a nice time in a canoe before."

But a deep roll of thunder gave a second warning and the horns took up their call again frantically.

Suddenly Dunleith shipped his paddle for an instant and putting up both hands answered in a long musical shout, then began to paddle again with long driving strokes that brought them soon to land.

There was no sign of Barry anywhere and they hurried up the hill, a hard climb with the wind driving down through the trees and twisting them like writhing creatures, so that it seemed momently some of them would fall.

One car had already started down the drive, a second pushed out as they came in sight, and the third was only lingering to give a message.

"Where is Blaine?" shouted Mr. Whitney leaning out of the car window, "he's got to drive that car. We're taking the chauffeur with us. Wasn't Blaine with you? He didn't go in any of the other cars."

"He was just down the hill," said Diana, looking startled. "I think he's not far away."

"Well, he'd better hurry up! We're driving to the Blue Goose Inn for dinner, everybody. It's only three miles from here. Blaine knows the way. Better hurry up, the storm's upon us."

Diana stood hesitantly looking back toward the woods, great drops of rain beginning to splash in her face, the lightning cutting vivid gashes in the blue-black heavens.

"Get in!" ordered Dunleith. "Quick! You'll get soaked!"

"But I ought to go back for Barry perhaps," said Diana, cringing as another flash of lightning was followed by a terrific crash of thunder.

"Get in quick!" ordered Dunleith again, taking hold of her arm firmly and fairly pushing her inside the shelter. "Hop in Pal. You stick by the ship and I'll run back for Blaine. He ought not to be far away."

"But you'll get soaked—!" said Diana with surprising unselfishness. "And—wait! Perhaps I ought to go! He may not come for you! He's sometimes—very—mulish!"

"I'll bring him!" said Dunleith slamming the car door shut and bolting for the woods.

Whatever methods the minister used, they were effective, for Diana, watching anxiously, quivering with fear at every fresh flash of lightning, presently saw two drenched figures, running through the torrent, collars turned up, heads bent to the driving wind.

They were both wet to the skin of course, but they climbed into the front seat, and Barry started the engine without looking back at the girl who had left him an hour before.

Dunleith sitting beside him watched his handsome sullen face and pondered.

The roads were abominable, and the driver did not seem to care what happened to his car. Sometimes it skidded almost off the road, but in due time they arrived, and found the rest of the party already at dinner, as gay as if there were no storm raging outside.

It did not take Dunleith long after he entered the place to discover that it was no spot he would have chosen. Glancing over at the corner where the little secretary had taken refuge he saw that she too was unhappy. But there was no escape at present while the storm raged, and they must make the best of it. The food was delicious, but the wine was flowing freely and Dunleith noticed that Blaine was taking

his friend's advice and filling himself up with it, "to
prevent taking cold." Dunleith himself drank a cup
of good hot coffee, and let it go at that. This was not
the first time he had been wet to the skin. There had
been worse things in France and Russia and Siberia
than a thunder storm at a picnic.

But the two wet ones had time enough to dry out
thoroughly before there came relief, for the storm
raged with great violence for nearly three hours, one
storm succeeding another, and each more violent
than the preceding one.

When they finally decided that it was safe to
start home every one was tired and cross.

Dunleith would have liked to make suggestions
about arrangements but there seemed no opportunity.

So he stuck to the boy, who by this time was one
succession of yawns, and bored to extinction:

"What do they see in all that dancing idea!" he
growled, "and getting themselves all tanked up! It's
the limit! But say, Pard, did you take notice, Diana
Dorne didn't drink to-night? She usually whoops it
up with the best of them. Mebbe that's cause she had
a fight with Barry. Or mebbe she's really fell for you,
Pard!"

"Oh, nothing like that, Kid," laughed Dunleith.
"Perhaps she's trying to help Barry. Perhaps she's
worried because he drinks so much."

"Aw, she never worries about anybody but herself!" announced the wise child. "Say, where do we
get stowed?"

"Wherever we are put, I guess, Kid."

But it appeared that some of the party had already
gone, and at the door stood a car with Caroline and
Fred in the back seat and Barry at the wheel.

"Diana's going in here," said Barry in gruff tones,
cupping his unsteady hands to light a cigarette.

Diana came out and looked around. The only other car was full.

"Get in here, Diana," said Barry gruffly as if he had the right.

Diana hesitated and drew back annoyedly, and quick as a flash Dunleith swung open the back door, jerked down the middle seat and almost shoved her into it, pushing Neddy after her into the other middle seat. Then he swung into the front seat himself by Barry and slammed the door.

"Who told you you might do that?" growled Barry. "What do you think you are doing anyway?"

But Dunleith paid no heed to the rudeness, and presently Barry started his engine and they were off.

The roads were still in terrible condition. The storm was by no means over. The night was black as pitch. Occasional distant rumblings, and startling illuminations over the whole sky showed that there might be another downpour at any moment.

Barry showed almost at once that he was not himself. He broke forth into song, and he lurched into the ditch at the side of the road, he recovered the crown of the road, and steered straight toward a tree. When the girls shrieked and protested he steered the car from one side of the road to the other, just to annoy them.

Dunleith sat stern and quiet beside him, watching his every movement. He saw Diana cower, and catch her breath. Once they skidded and turned almost completely around, and Barry began to curse the night and the storm and the roads.

When they came to the crossroads Diana begged Barry to take the longer right hand way.

"That hill will be awful to-night, you know," she said. "It's bad enough at any time."

"You think I can't drive down that hill to-night!"

railed Barry, "I'll show you what I can do," and turned sharply left, dashing down into a narrow steep cut whose condition was seldom good, and to-night was really treacherous. A wild torrent of water had cut a deep gully to the right of the road, down which the torrent was still madly rushing. There were three sharp curves in succession, with a gorge at the side fifty feet deep.

As the lights of the car were flung ahead on this frightful declivity, Barry stepped on his gas and plunged down.

"Oh, don't! Please don't! Barry, don't!" screamed the girls!

"Lemme alone!" blared Barry. "You think I can't drive! I'll show you or we'll all die in the attempt!"

He laughed a horrible vacant cackle, and stepped on the gas again. The car toppled wildly round one curve, then another, and was going straight for the chasm at a breakneck speed, when suddenly a strong arm knocked Barry's hand from the wheel, and veered it just enough to save them from an awful death.

Dunleith kept the car heading to the left of the road, and as they went off the slippery paving on to the rough shoulder he ground on the brakes. The sudden bumping frightened the girls again and they screamed in terror.

Barry, groping for his right senses, realized only that he had been rudely set aside, and began actively to protest.

Dunleith had no time to deal with him then, though his struggles to regain the wheel made driving twice as difficult. Barry, dazed and furious raised his hand to strike at the other man, when with one quick movement a soft silken scarf slid down over his face, and jerked his head back sharply.

With a strange glad thrill in his heart that Diana had been taking his part, Dunleith finally succeeded in bringing the car to a stand still.

"Now, get out!" he ordered.

Barry tried to protest in no pleasant language, but Dunleith threw open the door and pushed him from the front seat. He stood toppling crazily for a moment on the running board, and Dunleith got out and literally put him into the seat he had just been occupying. Then he went back to the driver's seat and took the wheel.

Slowly, carefully he piloted the car down the rest of the treacherous hill, and back to the highway safely.

"Well," said Caroline leaning forward when the excitement was past, "we'll have to tell Mamma she was mistaken. She said you didn't know how to drive a car. She said you never had a chance to learn. But that was simply great! Where did you ever drive before, John?"

"Oh, I drove a truck sometimes over in France," said John Dunleith casually. Then looking back to Caroline's escort he said: "Look out for Barry won't you? He's quite beyond looking out for himself."

At last they drove up to the house from which they had departed so gayly. Caroline rushed in to make known in a loud voice their narrow escape and Cousin John's marvelous rescue at the critical moment. Mr. Whitney came out to see about it, angry, excited, grateful. He put his arm on his young son's shoulder lovingly, hungrily, and Neddy looked up to his father's face with a wise understanding grin:

"Say, Dad, you oughtta have seen Cousin John handle that car! He certainly is one cracker jack driver!"

It was Dunleith who got Barry up to his room, quietly, by the back stairs, and put him to bed, and he did not linger downstairs to hear his praises sounded. He was sick at heart over the whole day. A girl like that and a young man like that throwing their lives away! A lily girl, who could look earnest and ask questions that showed her heart was stirred! A thoughtless, giddy butterfly of a girl who didn't know what it was all about. But would she tie her life to a young man already given over to drink? What a sad awakening there would be for her some day!

And over in her room Amory was putting away her wet garments, preparing for the night, and thinking what a day this had been! Oh, she was earning every penny of her salary by the hardest!

Down below in the library with the windows wide open, somebody had turned on the radio, and the voice of the announcer came out loud and clear:

"Ted Kingsley, the flier who set out at midnight Sunday night to make a non-stop flight to Nome and was reported to have passed over the city of Dawson at six this morning, his engine going strong, has not been heard from since and it is feared something has gone wrong with his radio. He is now ten hours over-due at Nome."

Amory dropped on her knees and began to pray.

CHAPTER XIII

Morning brought no better news.

A couple of mining camps in the Canadian Rockies

reported that they thought they heard a plane about midnight but it was not near enough for them to be sure. Down near Sitka there came one or two other rumors that an engine had been heard. But nothing had come through the air from the lost plane, and the gravest apprehensions were felt for young Kingsley whose genial grin was a nation wide joy, and whose former daring feats had made him a hero. There was a hint that rescuers were even now preparing to go in search of him. In Briarcliffe a pall suddenly settled down upon the house. Added to the fact that it was the day afterward and most of them were feeling the physical effects of a strenuous outing with no intervals of rest, the entire household was depressed by the terrible uncertainty concerning one who had been among them so gayly, but a few short hours before.

Barry came down late looking haggard and sullen. He smoked incessantly and scarcely answered when he was spoken to.

Most of the company resorted to cards as a quiet and decent manner of passing this time of solemn uncertainty. But there was no interest in the games, and finally Diana flung down her cards and got up.

"Count me out," she said. "I can't seem to put my mind on the cards. Here, you, Sam Marsden," looking at the young neighbor who had just dropped in, "you take my place."

Barry glared, but Diana went out of the room.

She went restlessly from room to room as if searching for some one, and then stepped out on the terrace.

Dunleith was down at the end of the garden sitting in a rose arbor with a book, and Ned not far away by the basin of the big fountain was working away at a miniature ship repairing its tiny sails.

Diana went straight down to the arbor, and appeared suddenly before Dunleith.

"What becomes of people when they die?" she asked abruptly without preamble. "Do they know anything afterwards? Do they—go somewhere?"

"Most certainly!" answered Dunleith with a quick lighting of his eyes.

"But, where do they go?"

"If they are Christ's they go immediately to be with Him."

Diana's eyes widened perplexedly.

"I don't believe—Ted—was—" she said sorrowfully. "He never talked about such things. I don't believe he ever thought anything about them."

"You can't ever tell when a soul may have met God and become His child. It takes only an instant for such a transaction to take place."

"You mean—if he knew—he was falling—he could do something about it—*even then?*"

Dunleith nodded.

"God is always close at hand. It does not take time to take God."

"But he would not know what to do," said Diana her eyes full of tears.

"God has ways of talking to souls that we do not understand. The Holy Spirit would show him what to do."

The tears were falling now, much to Diana's astonishment. She was not a crying girl, and she brushed them away almost angrily, and turned her face from him to hide them.

"Was he—very close—to you?" asked Dunleith with keen pity in his voice.

"Ted? Oh, no, but we've been pals since we could creep. It—just—seems—so awful—that's all!" she said dabbing her eyes with a gay little Paris handkerchief, and facing about with an attempt at a smile.

"But they have not given up hope yet," said Dunleith kindly. "Any one of a hundred different things may have happened to him. He may have had to come down in some lonely place where no one saw him, and his radio may be out of order Perhaps he'll turn up again and surprise everybody He may have stopped to sleep you know. That's the greatest danger really on those long flights that a man will fall asleep at the wheel. I imagine Kingsley has a lot of sense and if he found himself in danger of dropping off he would feel it was far more sensible to come down when he found a good landing place, and take a little rest before he went on A flier has to think of all sorts of things. Or, he may have come down to repair some of his machinery. I woudn't give up hope."

She looked at him curiously.

"You talk as if you knew all about it," she said.

"Well, I did quite a bit of flying when I was in the army," he said, "but nothing of course in the line that Kingsley has taken. Mine was only in the way of duty."

Diana stared at him.

"You're rather wonderful yourself, aren't you?" she said, and again for the third time Dunleith noticed a something genuine in her voice that made him look at her and wonder.

But he had no opportunity to reply for suddenly Barry appeared on the scene.

"We're going to ride, Di," he announced as if he had all right to order her doings. "Come on!"

Diana frowned but went, and Dunleith sat for a long time looking out through the rose draped arbor.

"Poor little girl!" he said to himself. "Poor little girl!"

The day wore on and the crowd still played cards,

the stakes growing higher and higher, as they felt the need of keener excitement to keep them from thinking what might be happening to Kingsley. Mrs. Whitney had tabooed the country club. She said it didn't look well for them to be over there having a good time publicly when their cousin was dead, perhaps. Mrs. Whitney's greatest anxiety always was how her actions would appear to an onlooking world. She did not relish the idea of a published snap shot of Caroline, perhaps, playing tennis at the country club, and labeled "Cousin of the lost flier taken this morning at Briarcliffe." One must be careful about those things. The family was going to be rather prominent just now, anyway, whatever was the outcome.

So the house party stayed at home, or drove quietly in country lanes. They did not dance, they did not even sing, they were not readers, so their only recourse was cards.

From time to time came messages over the radio, most of them speculations or false leads. A man down in the mountains of West Virginia had seen a strange plane flying over his head that acted as if it were in trouble, and had telegraphed the government. Another man in North Dakota had seen a man in flier's clothes driving madly by his house toward the north in an old Ford car, and he had sent a telegram to a New York paper. Every edition of the newspapers had some new theory as to what had become of Ted Kingsley.

By this time several searching parties had been organized and sent to the rescue, and Mr. Whitney had been closeted in the telephone booth for two hours arranging about a private rescue party that the Whitney family should send out after their beloved nephew.

"It will certainly look awfully well in the papers,

Henry," Leila Whitney had reminded him dabbing her eyes with her handkerchief. "You know people expect things of the family when they are at all able to do it."

"I don't give a hang what people expect!" roared the annoyed master of the house, hoarse with feeling, and furious at the telephone company for keeping him steaming in that booth so long. "I'm doing this for Ted! If there's anything that can save that kid's life I'm only too glad! As for the rest, poppycock! Spending a lot of money to make people think something of you that isn't so! That's your idea! But it isn't mine by a long shot. What is the matter with this infernal telephone? I wish you'd get out and let me alone. I can't hear what they say, Leila! Operator! Operator!"

Down on the terrace everybody was having an attack of nerves.

"Great Cats! I can't stand this!" said Susanne. "If the gloom doesn't lift I'm going to beat it! Everybody as long faced as a funeral director! Barry drinking himself to death and Diana gone fluey! I'm going where you're allowed to smile a little. What's one flier? He knew this might happen when he went, didn't he? Well, he went, didn't he? Well, then that's that! Let's live our lives and forget it!"

The next morning she sweetly professed to have a letter from her mother calling her home, and departed bag and baggage. But Mrs. Whitney promptly supplied her place by Mary Lou Westervelt, and the house party dragged itself along.

These were hard days for Amory. She could not understand herself. Why should a man whom she had seen but twice, and then only for a few minutes each, have taken such a hold upon her heart that she could think of nothing else? Of course the peril of even a stranger was a thing that stirred any one, but this was different. This man had taken a place in her life that no one had ever taken before, and his few words, especially his good-by over the telephone, rang over and over again in her ears as she went about her tasks.

She was glad that there was much work to be done. There were some invitations to be recalled; there were people calling constantly on the telephone to learn the latest news of Kingsley. She had schooled her voice to answer calmly, gravely, when they asked the inevitable question, "Do you think he is still alive?" As if anybody knew that! As if anybody could do anything but hope and fear. Why put these awful things into words that cut and harrowed?

Amory came and went as a part of the machinery of the household. She had come to be accepted as such now by the guests, and the daughters of the house. Since they saw that she did not presume upon the privileges that were granted her socially, they no longer resented her presence among them, almost as one of them. Yet she was never one of them, and she felt as aloof as if she were dwelling in another world, a sort of spirit world, where they could not see her, and thought as little of her as if she had been but a spirit.

She prayed continually for Gareth as she went about her work, or sat down just to think about it all.

When she wrote to Aunt Hannah and Aunt Jocelyn she shrank from mentioning the calamity that had overtaken the household in which she had come to abide for a time. Yet after long thought she decided that she should. Sometime something would be said, even if Aunt Jocelyn did not read the whole account in the papers, and notice that Kingsley was connected with the Whitney family. Yes, of course, there were the papers and she would have to talk about the occurrence or they would think it strange. So she wrote briefly of the sadness and anxiety everybody there was going through, and then after another pause to consider, she wrote:

He was here for a short time just before he left. He showed me how his engine worked, and I saw him fly away. He has nice merry blue eyes and is very pleasant, his smile is just like sunshine and he has brown curly hair with gold lights in it. Everybody here seems to be very fond of him! I suppose you have seen about his flight in the papers.

That was all, but she sat back as if she had written a biography, her hands cold and tremulous, her cheeks burning with consciousness. It almost seemed to her that it was blazoned across that letter, "He called me Darling when he said good-by!" Her heart throbbed wildly every time she remembered that. It seemed to have changed the relationship of everything in her world. Nothing would ever be quite the same again after that!

Yet, if he came back he would probably never think of it again. She hated to acknowledge to herself that such a thing could be possible, but she knew the world from which he came, knew the lightness with which modern young people look upon things that to her were sacred. How could she hope that there would be any following up of such a casual word flung out into the night across hundreds of miles on a mere wire, by a man who was saying goodby through her to his world, perhaps forever? Oh, she must not judge him! Yet she knew in her heart that if he should never return she would always hold that dear word as hers alone, and cherish it to the end of life. She knew, too, that there would never in the world be any one else like him for her.

And so she prayed, constantly, her petitions mixed

with thanksgiving for the little word he had given her at the last that all was right with him whatever came! Surely that meant that somehow he had found God. And her heart thrilled again at the wonder of having some of her prayers answered so quickly and so perfectly. Surely, he was hers in an especial sense, whatever came in life, even if she never saw him again—yes, and even if he came back alive and well, and still she never saw him again. All was in the Father's hands, and all would be well. She must always be happy and trust in that—whatever came.

Yet she would not have been human if she had not watched the papers anxiously, walking often to the village to get the latest edition; often stealing in to the radio when no one was by. For the radio was kept constantly turned on now at a point where news of the lost one would be likely to come. It spoke out weirdly whether any one was listening or not. The library where it was installed was almost wholly deserted by the young people, as if a corpse were lying there, but Amory found much comfort in lingering near with ears attuned to anything that might give hope that Gareth lived.

There came one terrible rumor, that a great light had been seen for a little while from a point on the coast of Alaska, looking off toward a small uninhabited island, and the fear grew into almost a statement, that the plane had caught fire and the pilot had perished. But rescuers immediately flew to investigate, and the story was not substantiated. No sign of any remains of a burnt plane were anywhere to be found within miles of the region named, and the matter was dropped from the calculations. Yet the rumor lingered as a tragic background for all the other rumors that followed. Day followed anxious day, and still no word came of the lost plane. The newspapers had almost omitted all mention of the matter, to make room for later thrills, and still the heaviness hung over the Whitney house.

One by one the guests had made excuses and gone away. Fred and Clarence were invited to a yachting party, and it was sailing sooner than they had expected. One girl's mother was ill, and another girl had to go home and get a dress fitted to be bridesmaid at a wedding. Barry Blaine lingered sullenly on, and one night late, when he had been deliberately drinking too much, he went down in the garden under the stars and had it out with Diana Dorne.

Blaine left the next morning, early, before any one was up. He left a note for Mrs. Whitney saying he had been called away, but every one had heard his loud words with Diana in the garden, though they could not hear her replies, and they all understood. He said he might return later, but the master of the house openly hoped he would not. And so the others all drifted away, one at a time, Mary Lou Westervelt lingering longer than the rest because she had come latest; all except Diana. She asked Mrs. Whitney if she might stay a few days longer. She said she liked it here, and had nothing much to do for another week. Of course Mrs. Whitney said she would be delighted to have her.

"She's just staying to carry out that infernal joke on John," said the master of the house when he heard it. "She's like a bull dog, when she once gets her little white teeth in any one she won't let go. She's not good enough for John, and she's too insignificant to be allowed to make him suffer."

"Suffer? Henry, what can you mean? How could Diana make your nephew suffer?"

"Humph! How could she? Don't ask me! Because every young man, no matter how sensibly he may be constituted otherwise, seems not to be able to keep from losing his soul sooner or later to every yellow eyelash that comes in his neighborhood. He's beginning to fall for her, I can see; and I don't like it! I wish she'd take her self and her pretty little curly head out of the neighborhood for good, John's worth too much to be allowed to be wrecked."

"The very idea, Henry! John has more sense than to think that Diana could possibly ever want to marry him! She wouldn't look at him!"

"Well, she's done a good deal of looking the last few days I should say," snorted her husband, "but I should like to know why she wouldn't look at my nephew? He's a long sight better than she is. And if you mean money I always meant that what should have been my sister's share of the estate would go to him. I didn't give it to him sooner because I didn't want him to get spoiled the way your nephew was by knowing he belonged to the idle rich."

"Now, Henry!" said Leila Whitney tearfully, "I wish you wouldn't speak of the dead in that way. I wish you would at least confine your ugly remarks to the living."

"Dead?" sniffed Henry. "So you count him dead now, do you? You said this morning that you were sure he was alive!"

"Well,—it begins—to look—that way!" sobbed his wife.

"Well, dead or alive Ted knows what I think of him, and it'll be all right with him even if he'd overheard it now. He understand what I mean."

The interview was abruptly terminated at that point by the arrival of the afternoon mail, and Leila Whitney made good her retreat before her husband would remember to bring up the subject again.

But Diana did not give cause for further criticism. She spent most of her time with Caroline and Doris, and openly kept aloof from Dunleith. Leila Whitney began to wonder whether possibly she might have overheard their conversation, and was trying to show them that she was not interested in the young minister.

The Sabbath came again, and the master of the house suddenly developed an interest in hearing his nephew preach. He ordered that the family should all attend church in a body. He said the car would be at the door in plenty of time, and that John was to go with them. But John ordered differently. He said he had promised to teach that class of boys again, so he and Neddy were driven down early, alone.

Barry had arrived again the night before, his coming as unexplained as his departure had been, but Diana had not received him with her usual graciousness. She was polite to him, that was all, and he fell into his sulks again.

"You needn't go to church you know, Diana," said Caroline to her guest, after the fiat had gone forth that the family must attend church in a body. "Dad won't mind what you do."

"Oh, I don't mind," said Diana lazily, "it will rather break the monotony you know."

"Don't try to keep her at home, Caroline," said her mother, "I quite agree with your father that we ought to go. It will be really expected of the family after what has happened, that we attend service somewhere you know, and of course since your cousin John is a regular minister no one would think it strange that we went to the chapel in the village instead of our regular church. It isn't as if we were in the city, either, you know. This church out here is only a summer one. I think it will look quite all right!"

So they went to church to hear John Dunleith, and Barry went also. There was nothing else for him to do unless he went home again, which he was not yet ready to do. He had been counting on having the morning in the woods with Diana.

But this time Diana went into the seat first and put herself away up at the end next the wall—for they were too late to get seats in the middle section of the little chapel—and Caroline and Doris came next. Barry had to content himself with a seat just behind them all so that his host might sit next to his wife. Seated thus he was able to get a continuous glimpse of Diana's face, and to read in it something more than the passing interest of a flirt, as she listened to the morning service. There seemed to be something awakened and alert, something wistful and new in the eyes of the girl whom he had grown to consider of late as his own property. Was there a new fineness there that he had not suspected before, a something restless, that was not going to be satisfied with the giddy, reckless life of the past? Was it that ass of a preacher that had fascinated her? They had all made a fuss over him since that night when he was half stewed and couldn't see the road anyway, but any one might have been in the same fix, and any good driver might have saved the situation.

But as he watched Diana's face during the service he was puzzled. The look in her face was not the usual one when she was getting a new crush on somebody. It was wistful, troubled, sad, utterly un-self-conscious, and that was something he never before remembered to have seen in Diana. She was always absolutely conscious of every pose she took, absolutely calculating about her clothes and her expression, and her actions. What had happend to her now? He must get her out of this atmosphere at once. Perhaps it was Ted! He had never taken Ted seriously, nor counted him even half a rival. Ted had always seemed to belong to everybody. He had always been so impersonal in his friendships. But perhaps Diana had really fallen for him more than they all knew! Well, he would get her away, whether it was Ted or the preacher. She was better off as far from Briarcliffe as possible. He would phone his aunt up in the Adirondacks to invite her there for the next week, and they would have a gay time and she would forget.

So he sat planning, hearing no smallest word of the sermon, thinking his own selfish thoughts.

Mr. Whitney listened to his nephew in amazement, frowned over some of the unusual things he was saying, remarked to himself that the boy seemed to know his Bible, for almost everything he said John read a confirmation in the little worn black Bible he held in his hand. Mr. Whitney looked around on the congregation noting their rapt attention and swelled with pride that *his* nephew was able to hold people like that.

"But they were very common people most of them," said Leila Whitney afterward when he remarked about it. "Oh, of course there were a few. The Desmonds were there. I've heard she makes a point of patronizing that chapel. It was built as a memorial to a son she lost in the war I think. Yes, and the Chesneys. Mrs. Chesney had on one of the new hats they are bringing over from Paris. I was reading about it last night, up from the face and down over one ear you know."

"One would think to hear you, Leila, that you had a hat down over both ears this morning!" remarked her husband disgustedly. "Where's my ash tray? Yes, I certainly was proud of a nephew that can preach like that. When we get back to the city I must see what I can do to get him into some big church. He deserves to succeed. He's made himself you know, no big fortunes financing him in college, no big crowds lauding every turn he makes, no newspapers photographing his grin, and broadcasting it all over the earth—!"

"I don't see why you always have to hit at my poor dear Theodore!" began Leila Whitney, "now that he's in trouble too—!"

"How do you know he's in trouble?" snapped her husband. "I wasn't hitting at him. Ted's all right in spite of the things you and his poor dear mistaken grandfather did to him. But there, there, there! Leila, for mercy's sake don't turn on the faucets again, I can't stand any more to-day. I haven't been to church in a year and it's a strain. You must be considerate! Whose car is that driving up? Is that that unspeakable cur of a Marsden again? Say, are you going to stand him around Doris? Because I'm not if you are. I think I'll go out and shoo him off to-day. We've had him all the week, and it's time we had a little let up," and he passed out of the range of his wife's tears, knowing that they would cease as soon as her audience was removed; knowing also that he had just given her a counter irritant which would soon make her forget her other grievance.

Amory in her room as usual, where she spent most of her time, could not help but hear the dialogue, and was ready both to laugh and to cry. How true it was that wealth did not always bring happiness. And yet these two people who quarreled most of the time that they were together had both been young once, and probably thought they were in love with one another. How had they lost the vision of life? How infinitely happier than they was dear Aunt Hannah lying on her bed of pain and submitting sweetly to whatever the dear Lord sent her!

How much these two people needed the peace which passeth understanding that John Dunleith had been preaching about to-day! Had they taken in any of its wonderful meaning at all? Their talk did not sound as if they had.

And then her heart beat back to the same question that had been crying out silently day after day ever since the silence had dropped down between Gareth Kingsley and the world. Would the mystery never be solved this side of heaven? Would they never find out what became of him? Was the world really so large that a man in a big plane like that could actually be lost utterly, and never found?

CHAPTER XIV

WHEN Gareth Kingsley at last came out of that long swoon which the shock of his fall had caused he opened his eyes and looked about him. For a long eon he had no thoughts. It was not even a question with him where he might be or why he was there. He was merely getting accustomed to being alive again.

Gradually, however, his surroundings detached themselves from each other, bit by bit and came to his attention. There were little close dark walls about him everywhere, composed of frames filled with smooth dark panels. One of the panels must be open for he felt crisp cold air coming in. He presently became aware of light shining sharp and keen across him, and realized that he was lying slumped in a queer uncomfortable heap and yet could do nothing about it.

The first thing that really recalled him to himself was the wheel. Ah! He knew that. He had not sat for long hours clinging to that faithful wheel to forget it! This was the cabin of his plane. And he had been going—where?

Bit by bit it all came back to him, and then in a flash he remembered what had happened. And now he was—here! Where was here?

Slowly, carefully he tried himself, first a finger at a time, then his arm, and then he tried to raise himself, but found pain in every joint. Was his leg broken, or was it only sprained? He could not tell. But he must find out. He must do something at once. Perhaps he could repair the damage done to his plane and proceed after the first soreness was over. He had learned long ago on the football team, and later in the army, that the cure for sore muscles was action. Perhaps this was only pain from his cramped muscles. He would force himself to get out. Besides, he must discover where he was before night came and shut him in. How long was it since he had lost consciousness? Only a few minutes, or had he been wasting precious hours? He looked at his watch, but it had stopped! That meant he had no time!

Painfully he drew himself up to the seat in the cockpit, for the shock of the landing had slumped him on the floor. Painfully he studied his chart and compass, but they seemed to mean nothing, and the glass over the compass was shattered in minute particles.

He reached for his stores and ate a little food, but hunger seemed to have passed from him. However it revived him. He drank a few drops of the precious water in his canteen, and then realized that the thing he must do at once was to find out his whereabouts as nearly as possible and radio his situation to the people who were waiting anxiously to know. That he had failed of his perfect purpose, as planned from the start was a foregone conclusion, but he might yet be not so far from his first goal. If he could get out and get his oil line fixed up he might be able to make Nome yet, that is unless the oil had all leaked out.

Painfully he made a supreme effort and got himself out of his cabin, and into a cold bright world that he did not know.

Never before had he dreamed such ice, such clear still beauty of whiteness set in queer, cold blue. He stared about him, one hand holding to the side of his boat, and felt his strong limbs tremble under him, and his broad shoulders slump with weariness and exhaustion.

Nowhere in any direction could he see anything but white ice heaving and churning, or towering up in forbidding crystal mountains against the bluest sky he ever saw, a cold blue sky.

He ventured to hobble off a few steps and found he could still stand alone, though it hurt him amazingly to do so. He looked at his poor proud plane and found its landing gear torn off. Even though he might repair the oil line, could he ever get her free without help? From all he had read of icebergs, this must be one. Below the tail of the plane ran a wide crevasse like a black yawning chasm. When that grew wider as it seemed as if it might do at any moment what would be the effect on his plane? Would it sink into those everlasting cold depths, and carry him with it? Would a grave in the frozen seas be any worse than a grave on shore?

Then it came to him. He was a child of God! He had been born again. On sea or land, or beneath the ice, God knew and cared where he was. This was all in the plan, the good plan!

And what message should he send back to the

world who had sent him here, from this Nowhere to which he had come? It wasn't necessary to make a great fuss, and get everybody writing up fool headlines. Better make it snappy, practical!

"Oil line broken, made landing on iceberg, can't tell how far from shore, ought to be somewhere near Nome. Landing gear gone, compass acted queer. Need help for repairs. Don't worry!"

That would sound all right. Now, if he could get back into that cabin without too much pain he had better get that message off as soon as possible.

But the radio lay dead. Something gone wrong with that too! He examined and found the batteries shattered by the blow when the ship's nose crashed into the ice. So! That was that!

He was here alone with God!

He tried his engine. That was gone dead too! By and by when he was rested he would look into it and see if there was anything he could do about that. When help came—of course they would come— That was one thing he could depend upon—that they would come—always supposing they came in time before the iceberg parted and let him down in the icy waters— So when help came he would want to be in good shape to fly as soon as his oil line was repaired. They would bring him oil of course, if his was all gone. Meanwhile that deadly sleep had come down upon him again. Didn't that prove that it wasn't long since he had landed?

He made himself as comfortable as possible and slept. How long, he did not know. It was daylight when he went to sleep, it was still daylight when he awoke. He knew that at this season of the year there was almost continuous daylight, so he could judge nothing by that. He would set his watch at an hour and see what happened. But his watch acted queerly and ticked off a few paces, then stopped! Ha! Was even his watch smashed?

Well, he had passed to a place where time meant nothing any more! That was startling! Then if he ever did get back he would not be able to give any definite report. His experience would have to count for nothing on the records. That was hard luck, but why worry?

He began to look into his stores and examine the different parts of his ship. He got out some of his tools, and feeling rested and less sore in his muscles climbed out upon the ice again, rejoicing that he did not have to count a broken leg among his troubles. With the few tools in his kit he went at his plane with the idea of dislodging it from the ice. Perhaps he could construct some kind of a frail boat out of the materials of the plane still undamaged. But he soon found that it would take power more mighty than any at his command to dislodge the plane, and the idea of making a boat and attempting to launch it single-handed was impossible. But since his ship could not fly it was well that it had a strong harbor for the present at least.

Finding that he could walk more comfortably he took a short tramp around his prison, never venturing very far in any direction from the plane lest some sudden crevasse separate him from even that shelter.

He got out his glasses, and looked earnestly in every direction, but still there was not a sign of anything but whiteness against the deep cold blue. The grandeur of it all impressed him tremendously and filled him with awe. This was his Father's world. He was glad he was seeing this far part of it. He was not anxious to remain here long, for there were strong drawings in other directions, but since he was here he would take it in, and store it up in his memory. He felt he could never again be quite so blind to the wonders of earth since he had looked upon all this empty beauty, with no one by to see except himself.

And now he began to calculate just how long he could wait alive upon this floating island.

It was not so bitter cold as he had supposed it would be. In fact it was warmer than flying high in a gale of hail and storm. But when the night should come down, even though it were brief, or when a terrible northern wind should blow as he knew it did up here sometimes, could he hold out for even an hour or two?

Certainly he ought to get at that engine and see what it needed. Get at that oil line and find out if it could be repaired and whether the oil was all gone, or there was a little, just enough to warrant his flying off and trying to get to mainland—always supposing he could get off!

So he went to work.

But the oil line showed at once that there was no hope there, even if he repaired it, for the oil was gone entirely, and a slimy black line showed where the last had leaked out and drained toward the crevasse. He went and gazed down into the heaving blackness below that crack, and wondered if there might be some way to gather again that oil that had slipped down on the water, but gave it up as impossible.

He tinkered awhile at the oil line, but did not accomplish much. It would need help beyond his own to get that plane in working order. He worked at the engine a while, cleaning and polishing certain parts, and making right what he could, as one will pet a cherished animal. It was good to be standing on a firm foundation, and petting up the old plane, just as he did on the flying field at home, trying to pretend it was not smashed—only in need of minor adjustments; trying to feel that land was just around the corner and help was coming soon through the air.

But when he turned around and saw that still emptiness in every direction his heart failed him.

He thought of the morning he left Briarcliffe, and the little girl with the blue eyes and the Testament, who wanted him to be "saved." Well, he was saved—so far—saved from immediate death- saved also for eternity, for he believed now with all his heart that God had accepted him in Christ. He had contemplated a swift death, and believed that he would have been safe forever under those circumstances, but he had never contemplated this utter desolation, this wild waste of living death. How long did it take to starve to death? Or would freezing come before that? He had rations for serveral days and with careful economy could make them last twice as long. But safety did not depend upon himself. It did not depend upon that little box of stores in the cabin. He had given himself to God, and God could make him safe here upon this island of ice alone between sea and heaven as well as i he had been driven to earth in a storm and his body suffered swift death. He had put himsel into God's hands, and promised to trust Him, and this was what being safe meant. It did not necessarily mean getting back to Briarcliffe to see those blue eyes of Amory again. But it did mean that some day with his own eyes he could see God, and see Amory again too.

These things were borne in upon him gradually as he stood at last, his tools laid down, his arms folded helplessly and looked up.

"God, I am yours!" he said aloud, slowly, solemnly, like a consecration. "Do with me what you want to do."

He stood for an instant with bowed head, as if

waiting before the One whom he had addressed, and
then he looked up with his old smile:

"And now I have time to read that little book!"
he said aloud again, and felt that it was pleasant to
hear his own voice in this empty loneliness. "I will
read it through!"

He climbed into his cabin, and read for hours,
until sleep claimed him again; and when he awoke,
he read again.

A queer brief night with a sunset effect in it,
hovered over the place now and then. He had no
means of telling how long it lasted nor how often
it came. He could only judge that it was an Arctic
night.

Several of these succeeded one another. He made
a notch with his knife on the cabin window sill lest
he should forget how many there had been.

Life began to settle down into a routine. He doled
out his food in tiny quantities, counting how long
it would last. He planned a schedule so that he would
not get into a rut. He must keep fit. He must have
exercise. He walked so many times around his prison
every little while. He took setting up exercises, and
drilled himself as if he were in the army. He laughed
aloud, and tried to keep up good cheer. He slept a
good deal because he knew that sleep often did in
place of food, and he must be careful with that
precious little store of food that was growing less and
less so rapidly. How many more midnight suns
would rise and set before it would be entirely gone?
Were there fishes in this queer icy sea, fishes that
were fit for food, fishes small enough to catch with
crude tackle. He even rigged up a line with a bent
pin, put a bit of canned meat on for bait, and tried
fishing in the crevasse, but nothing came of it.

No birds flew over his cold white harbor that he
might have shot. Nothing, nothing, but what he had

brought with him! Nothing but the little book. For he was reading it through as he had said, and it was teaching him wonderful things.

There was perhaps no spot in His wide universe where God might have tucked His new born child, where he would have been so shut down to feed upon the Word of Truth, and be led by the Holy Spirit, as on that wide white island of Nowhere, shut in by the eternal sky and the heaving icy sea.

Day by day he watched the sky, the sea, but no ships appeared in sea or air. Day by day he awoke with new hope and looked out, but still that stretch of cold blue and white, and only himself and God. For now he had come to feel that God was very real, and quite near at hand.

He had finished the little book. He had read it through again, reading it book by book this time, and conning it till much became plain that he had not noticed the first time. Among other things that he had found was a statement, made several times, that "This same Jesus" should come again, and that with Him were to come "the dead in Christ." That was a strange statement. He had never heard that Christian people believed that, but it was good. It was reasonable. It certainly was interesting to think about. "The dead in Christ." Well, he would be one of those dead! It would not be many days now till some night, some short queer Arctic night, he would lie down, with a gnawing hunger working at his vitals, and in the morning he would not wake up. Then he would be one of the dead in Christ!

He had not expected to have time to contemplate his own death this way, but since he had found this book and learned all it had to teach it was not an unhappy thing. "And the dead in Christ shall rise first." That was good. He would be coming with the

Lord! "Then we which are alive"— That would likely be Amory if it happened soon— Or, if she were among the dead in Christ they would be coming together. That would be great! It was great however it was!

Much he dreamed about these things, and thought what he would say when he should meet her—in the air— Why! She would be flying with him then, real flying, with wings that did not break!

Often now as he read, his thoughts trailed off into dreams, and sometimes he thought Amory came and talked with him about the little book, and what she thought it meant.

He was eating so little now that he felt very weak, and did not care to walk around his island. It hardly seemed worth while. He must save his strength to read. He wanted to know all he could about what God had said before he went to meet Him. He could understand now why he had been allowed to live so long, that he might learn and be ready for the other world.

There came a morning when he had eaten the last bite of food and swallowed the last mouthful of water. It had hardly seemed worth while to bother about them, for what could those little mites of susenance do but prolong the agony of the final separation of soul and spirit? But he duly swallowed them.

He was chilly much of the time now, chilled to his very bones. He had never known there could be such cold as came rushing over him at intervals, when he was not burning hot. Most of the time now, even when he was cold he was hot too, fiery hot; hot in his head and his hands, and sick and hot in his stomach that had long ago ceased to want food. Only that heat and terrible cold succeeding one another, and that terrible weakness, and restless moving of his limbs that were so tired—too tired to move, yet had to. He could scarcely believe that one who had felt so strong all his life could feel so weak now.

It was days since he had thought to watch the sky. He had been too engrossed with the little book, and with getting ready to go above. He slept much at intervals, and later in the day—or was it the following day? He could not remember a night. He roused with the burden that he must leave some message behind.

Feebly he felt in his pocket for his knife, and began to scratch rude letters on the window frame. His breath came fast, and the effort to sit up was almost too much. Perhaps some day they would come and find the plane and read the letters of that phrase that rang in his head. They would put them in the paper, and she would know. Amory would understand!

He would have liked to begin it with the word "Darling" so she would know it was meant for her, but that might be to expose her to embarrassment, his fevered brain reasoned, so he would only put the other words. But she would understand!

With a great effort he scratched three words, then he was seized with a terrible dizziness. Fighting against it with all his iron will he finished the last word, crudely,—weak—so weak—!

"GARETH, CHILD OF GOD!" it read. He had finished the name of God. His hand dropped!

"Oh, I can't make it!" he cried. "But you will understand—*Darling!*"

His hand fell feebly on his knee, slipped off and drooped limply, and a shudder ran through his whole frame.

"D-a-r-l-i-n-g—!" he whispered.

CHAPTER XV

THE morning they found the plane the radios all over the land rang with the news, broke in through jazz, and daily dozens, and recipes for making pies, interrupted grave lectures on abtruse themes, and talks to mothers on how to bring up their children!

Kingsley's plane had been found at last wedged in an iceberg floating in the Arctic Ocean, far above the most northern line that Kingsley had expected to take. Its oil line was broken, its engine gone bad from a crash, its radio dead, its landing gear broken, and the food supply gone, but Kingsley himself was nowhere to be seen, though the entire region had been carefully searched and would continue to be searched for miles around.

A careful examination of the plane for some sort of message from the flier had revealed nothing save a mysterious sentence scratched crudely on the inside of the cabin window.

"Gareth, child of God!"

It was supposed that the flier might have abandoned his plane hurriedly, and tried to reach the mainland over the ice, possibly before the iceberg had separated itself far from the coast, or had drifted so far out to sea; but it was a hazardous chance to take, and he had probably met his death in the icy waters.

Neither newspaper nor radio announcer offered

any solution of the mysterious sentence carved on the cabin window, though the unexplained sentence caused much useless discussion and surmise.

But to Amory, coming upon the paper before any one else in the house was about, the words spoke volumes. This was a message all her own and he had sent it that way so others would not understand!

Trembling between radiance and tears she stood and read the entire column, looked earnestly at the picture that was used at the head, so lifelike, with that grin, just as he had looked when he tried to convince her they were properly introduced. He seemed to be looking at her now and trying to make her understand:

"Gareth! Child of God!"

That meant that he had found the Lord before he died! It meant perhaps that he had read her little book, and learned to know what it meant!

Later in the day she secured that paper and read in other columns about the desolate spot where the plane rested, read and tried to picture it all out, and live over the time he might have spent there, carving that sentence for her.

When she had finished she laid the paper on the bed, and dropping down beside it put her face against the picture, and whispered softly: "Darling!"

After a little she got up and went and searched out the little silver wings, and pinned them inside her dress over her heart. They were hers, now, forever, by his last will and testament.

Then with an exalted look upon her face, like one who had been through great joy and great sorrow hand in hand, she went about her work again. It would not be necessary now to explain all this to Aunt Hannah and Aunt Jocelyn. They would never understand, and it was too sacred to be talked over

If Gareth had lived—! But now—it was her secret to keep till the day they met again.

The world went wild with mourning for a few days of course. Bells were tolled solemnly, buildings were draped with black, flags were hung at half mast, even services were held, after a due time had elapsed for the possibility of finding a trace of the missing man. Mrs. Whitney bought some new and becoming black dresses, and told the girls they really ought not to plan to give any dances for at least three months.

A service was held in one of the fashionable churches of Briarcliffe, instigated by a far-seeing official who wanted to curry favor with the Whitneys, and who talked fervently of wanting to honor "one of our very own of whom we are proud."

The church was draped in black with masses of costly flowers.

There was tender fitting music along the line of heroism and the triumph of the conqueror; a man of nation-wide reputation was imported from New York to pronounce an eloquent eulogy on the brave young hero who laid down his life in the cause of science and Progress with a capital P. He ranged him unquestionably with the great of the ages, such as Abraham Lincoln, Theodore Roosevelt, and even Jesus Christ. The chancel was a mass of white lilies and glowing roses, and before the altar was laid a crown of olive leaves with the victor's palm. It was all most beautiful and perfect, and Leila Whitney heavily draped in black, leaning on her husband's arm, walked with stately measure, her black bordered handkerchief to her eyes, and her family and guests walking behind.

But at home in her room, quietly beside her bed knelt the little secretary, praying!

It was the evening of that day when they had all gone to the service to please Mrs. Whitney.

John Dunleith was down in the arbor with his book beside him. He had been working on his next Sabbath's sermon, but when the dusk came down he threw aside his book and threw back his head against the rustic trellis, looking out where the gorgeous sunset still lingered softly in the sky.

Ned had gone, much against his will, to see a boy who was visiting a neighbor. He would not have gone if the neighbor had not telephoned his mother, and his mother insisted.

There were lights in the house, and the general air of relief that comes when a funeral is over and the family are returned from the grave. The voices of Doris and Caroline could be heard laughing without restraint again, unrebuked. They were all glad to have the incident finished and their duty of mourning complete.

John sat thinking of his cousin whom he had seen but seldom and remembered only as a cheerful lovable companion. He was wondering what the end of that gay life had been.

Up in the branches of the trees above there were soft little murmurings of birds settling for the night, nestlings crowding one another for more space under a wing. Little insects spoke in sleepy voices among the grass, and a tree toad chimed out like a bell. John Dunleith sat listening to it all, and heard too, a soft indefinable stir among the flowers like some one in quiet garments moving down the path, and before he saw her he knew who it would be.

Diana had kept much away from him for the last few days. Only at meals he had seen her, and then she sat at the other end of the table and talked very quietly. She had not addressed a word to him nor looked his way for several days.

Now she came slowly down the garden path, her head drooping, her whole attitude most humble.

She came straight to the arbor as if she had seen him even in the darkness, and pausing in the doorway she spoke in a low clear voice.

"Mr. Dunleith, I have come to confess something to you!" There was utmost sweetness and humility in her tone.

John Dunleith sprang to his feet at once.

"Sit down," he said, and then pleasantly, as she dropped into the arbor bench, "I am no priest, Miss Dorne. Why should you confess to me?"

"Because," she said looking down at her white hands clasped nervously together, and speaking with shame in her voice, "because it was against you I— sinned!"

He watched her gravely, eagerly, glad that the darkness hid the tenderness that must shine in his eyes, but he said nothing.

"I am ashamed— Oh, so much ashamed—" she went on. "I have come to understand what you are now, and now I see how terrible this will appear to you, this thing I tried to do to you. You haven't any idea how hard it is for me to tell you just what it was I did."

"Don't try," said John Dunleith. "It will be all right with me—"

"But no," she said quickly, "I must tell you. I cannot rest until you know it all. I have been outrageous! I got up a plot before you ever came, to drive you away! I had no malicious intent of course, it was to be only a practical joke. We didn't want you here because you were religious. We thought you wouldn't fit. And I—offered—"

Dunleith lifted his hand in protest.

"Spare yourself, please. I know all about it, and it was forgiven before you spoke."

"You know all about it?"

Diana lifted a white frightened face for a moment and stared at him through the darkness. "But how could you know?"

"Neddy overheard, and came to me with the tale the day I got here," he said lightly, trying to laugh it off as if it were of no consequence.

"Oh!" said the girl and dropped her face into her hands, sitting still and suffering in the soft rose perfumed darkness. He put out his hand and touched the border of her white floating dress.

"Don't!" he said, "it does not matter now!"

"Oh, but it does!" she said lifting her miserable eyes to his. "You don't understand. There is more to it than that. Neddy wouldn't have understood either. I planned to make you fall in love with me. I have done it before with other men, and I thought it would be a pleasant pastime. I planned—I actually planned—to—pretend to—be good—to get you to sort of convert me—if I couldn't do it any other way—! And when I found what you were I was angry that I could not conquer you. I had never seen a man like you before."

She stopped and dropped her face in her hands again and he could see her shoulders heaving as if she were suppressing sobs.

He rose and came toward her.

"I knew all that—Diana!" he said tenderly, and laid his hand on her bowed gold head like a blessing.

The quivering shoulders grew steady, and the girl's breath was held, as if she were afraid the blessing would leave her.

"I don't see how you can ever forgive me!" she said at last in a low penitent tone. "A man like you— for me to presume—I don't see how you ever can!"

"It is because I love you, Diana," he said simply with rare depth of earnestness in his voice. "You see, you did work your purpose, after all, little one. You did make me fall in love with you."

She quivered beneath his hand.

"Even though you knew how vile I was?"

"Even though I knew!"

"But I wasn't fit for you to love!" broke forth the penitent voice again. "I don't deserve that you should speak to me!"

"That has nothing at all to do with it," said the man sitting down beside her and drawing her close to his side with a strong protecting arm. "Diana, I love you! Don't you see how love covers it all? I love you next in the world to my Lord, and every day since I saw you first, and knew what you were trying to do, I have been praying for you. And the more I prayed for you the more tenderly I loved you. Don't you see how these human relationships are just beautiful pictures of God's love for us?"

"Oh," said Diana suddenly, "If I should pray— if you should pray for me—do you think He would let me be born again the way you preached last Sunday?"

"He certainly would. You have only to accept Him, and the thing is done."

"And—when—if—He comes to take you away— in the clouds the way you said He was coming pretty soon, would He let me go too?"

"He most assuredly would, you precious child!"

"Then let's ask Him now," said Diana softly.

He folded his arms close about her and with her face against his he prayed for her, and for himself, and for them both, and then sealed it with a kiss that made her know what it meant to be really loved by a man like this one.

Neddy, released at last from his social duties, hurrying in search of his comrade, came rubber-shod to the garden, and heard the voice of prayer.

He stopped stealthily, listening, and heard such words as reached the heart of even a child who was not supposed to understand; heard too the kiss that sealed the covenant, and turned with stricken, awe-filled eyes and stole away more silently than he had come.

"Good night!" he murmured to himself when he had attained the seclusion of one of his boyish haunts behind the garage where nobody ever came, "good night! That's the end of cousin John! But I guess the joke's on Diana after all! She thought she was stringing him, but he got her! How'll she make out cooking dinner for a missionary in Africa while he's out killing lions, I wonder?"

When Diana came into the house that night she was wearing on the third finger of her left hand a quaint old ring of twisted yellow gold in which was set one magnificent ruby. Dunleith had kept it with him since ever his mother was taken away. It had been her engagement ring.

Caroline noticed it and looked in wonder. Doris saw it and spoke right out.

"Great Cats! Diana, are you really going to Africa? What'll you do if a cannibal comes and tries to eat you?"

"I'll send for you to come and visit me," said Diana, looking up with pink cheeks that no longer needed any rouge to make them beautiful.

"But you don't mean that you are going to stand for that missionary stuff, do you?" asked Doris in amazement. "You won't have to, you know. I heard Daddy say he was going to get John a big church in New York this winter."

"John doesn't want a big church in New York, Dorrie dear, and neither do I. We are going to Africa to do some real work for God, and I'm proud that John thinks I can help him!"

"Great Cats! Diana, how you have changed!" said Doris and sat and stared at her for full five minutes without speaking.

"Well, there must really be something in it after all, if it can do that to *you*," she said at last with a sigh, and taking her tennis racket went off to the country club, pondering.

CHAPTER XVI

WHEN the knife fell from Gareth's nerveless fingers it struck against the cover of an empty biscuit tin, and went clattering inside, the cover rattling noisily after it; but Gareth lay still and did not move.

All day long there had been loud rending sounds like cannon booming at intervals, but Gareth had not heeded them, perhaps he had not heard them, so intent was he upon his work. And why should he hear that knife rattling into the empty biscuit tin, now that he had passed beyond such trivial things?

But out beyond that pile of rending ice, beyond which Gareth had not had the strength to look for many a day, there rode a little boat of walrus skin, and in it two eskimos with sharp ears attuned for strange sounds, in their wild still blue and white world.

The two looked at one another questioningly, and one pointed. The other nodded and turned the boat swiftly, skillfully, in the treacherous tide. Silently, with small bright eyes watching, they paddled their boat, finding a pathway where the ice had broken and cut great lanes like black rifts. Swiftly they slipped between big cakes of ice, as easily as one walks down a quiet hall, and without a sound the walrus boat arrived with its two fur-clad occupants beside the great ice island where the dead plane lay a prisoner.

Obeying a stealthy paddle the boat came to a standstill while the two stood up open mouthed and gazed at the great bird lying there with its silver wings outstretched, helpless.

The younger of the two eskimos began to speak in a low growl, under his breath, pointing to the plane, then lifting both his furry arms, flapping them like a bird, and pointing up. He had heard of an airship. Perhaps had seen one. He was telling his comrade about it.

The other nodded slowly, still gazing, awe struck.

They stood for a long minute more gazing, with heads atilt, in a listening attitude, then the young one spoke in a low tone again, and stepping softly from the boat climbed up the bank of frozen snow to the side of the plane and gazed again. Almost at once he discovered Gareth, and coming close watched him intently for an instant. Was he dead? He climbed closer and bent his head listening, watching this strange bird-man cautiously. Then suddenly he straightened up and called something to the other man in the boat, who made fast his bark, and came swiftly, going through the same process of listening, watching, caution. There ensued an argument, but the end of it was they pulled and hauled at Gareth till they got him up and out of the cockpit, and down on the snow. Then they carefully went through the cabin, and picked up all they could find, nodding knowingly when they came to the knife in the biscuit tin, their quick eyes taking in the newly cut letters on the wood of the cabin.

They made a trip to the walrus boat with all the trifles they had found, and then picked up the big man. Puffing, pulling, lifting, at last they managed to get him down the bank and into their boat. There he lay on the bottom inert and unconscious. He looked like a dead man. One of the two eskimos evidently thought he was dead.

There was scarcely room for the owners of the boat when they were ready to start, but they managed to get in, and began their long silent journey back to land, the elder man occasionally looking stolidly at Gareth lying so still and white. He chattered something to his mate, shaking his head and pointing.

After perhaps an hour's hard pulling they reached a white stretch of coast that was scarcely distinguishable from the sea of ice, and wended their way cunningly into a cove, where they beached with some difficulty their queer boat, and turning toward a strange hut, covered over with snow, called in a loud raucous voice.

There was a tiny thread of smoke coming out of the top of the snow mound that was a house, and presently from a small hole or door beneath out came two more little creatures, a young man and an old woman, and hurried down to the boat.

They carried Gareth between the four of them, and got him inside the hut. They laid him on a kind of mat on the floor. They felt his face, listened to his heart, and chattered above him enough to kill any two men, and then the old woman brought a cup of something hot and began to try to feed him.

He could not swallow, and at first they were not sure that even a drop had gone down his throat, but they kept patiently at their task, and at last they began to hope that a little of the warm fluid had been taken.

They chafed his hands and feet, they plied him

with all their native remedies, which would have
been laughable indeed to Gareth if he himself had
been there; and at last after three hours they were
rewarded with a slow quivering sigh.

They took off his queer helmet, and unfastened the
strange coat that seemed so heavy. They piled logs
on the fire that was built on the floor in the middle
of the room and they did their ignorant best to make
him comfortable.

Every hour they fed him a few more drops of the
warm broth, and were glad when they found he was
trying to swallow. But he did not open his eyes, nor
seem to know anything, and now he was growing
hot, very hot, and beginning to toss and moan.

There was no doubt in the minds of the small
anxious men and one woman but that the sick man
was very ill indeed, but they did not relax their vigi-
lance for a moment, even though it looked for days
as if there was no hope. Day after day the fever held
Gareth in its clutches, and because the people who
were caring for him were most ignorant, and because
his vitality had run very low during the long wait
on the iceberg with almost no food, it ran its course
with little to hinder. Day after day, hour after hour
his life hung in the balance, and sometimes it seemed
to the old woman who hovered over him that his
breath was gone.

And all the time Amory was bearing him up in the
arms of prayer, knowing not if he were yet alive, she
prayed continually, "Lord if he is alive, keep him
safely, bring him back!"

One day the fever left him, and he was very weak.
They thought he was gone more than once, as they
tried to make him eat. They tried to make him more
comfortable, and then sat in a solemn little fur circle
around their smoky fire, and watched him, wondering if he would ever open his eyes. They discussed

who he was and where he came from, and then went patiently on caring for him.

Only his splendid constitution kept him alive from day to day and brought him finally to the day when he opened his eyes and looked around the room.

The old woman with her cup of queer broth hovered between his vision and the roof of snow, and he focused his dazed eyes on her round greasy face framed in its scraggly fur fringe, and wrinkled his weak lips into a grin. The same grin that the papers had broadcasted from coast to coast he gave to the old woman in the snow hut who was bringing him back from death's door.

That grin was all he did that day. He swallowed the spoonfuls of queer tasting stuff they put into his mouth, but he did not open his eyes again until the next morning. Perhaps he preferred to dream he was still back in his ship waiting for help to come.

There was great excitement the next morning when he opened his eyes again, and gave another grin, looking from one to another of them.

They bustled about him, murmuring queer vowels and consonants, and he only grinned, but they liked it. White man very merry, thought they.

It was several hours later that he began to try to get something across to them. They stood around him and tried to puzzle out his meaning.

His voice was very weak, not at all like the big hearty cheer that used to be his natural tone. He said something to them which had they understood they could not have heard because it was so faint and far down in his throat. They jabbered at him and gesticulated, but they got nowhere at all, and he was weak, and so tired. At last, he managed to lift one finger, and turn his sick eyes toward his coat which was hanging on a pole that stood against the wall of snow.

Their eyes gleamed intelligently, and they brought him the coat, and now he tried to reach to the pocket when they laid it beside him. With weak fingers that would not obey his direction he touched the breast pocket and was thrilled to feel the Testament still there. They saw what he wanted, took the package out, and gave it to him. He smiled, a tired grin, and then with almost superhuman effort he motioned them to take the envelope, and made a feeble sweep with his arm to indicate far away. "Post Office!" he whispered faintly and dropped his eyelids shut over the effort. He thought that he was dying, and Amory would not get her Testament.

The eskimos took the package and studied it curiously, chattering among themselves and nodding. Then the elder man pointed to the younger men, and motioned far, handing them the letter.

Gareth opened his eyes with worry in them, and saw one of the men preparing to go out, fixing up as for a journey, and they nodded to him and motioned to his letter. Perhaps they understood. Anyhow he could do no more. He grinned a feeble thanks and closed his eyes again. What an effort that had been! How nearly detached from his body he had become! Think how he used to fly in the air, to drive a car, and play polo! Soon he would be gone!

He thought he heard a chanting over his head, "Child of God— Name of the Father!—Name of the Son!—Name of the Holy Ghost.—Gareth— Child of God!"

He slept, and murmured in his sleep, "Amory, Darling!"

The old woman hovered over, gave him something to swallow and he slept again.

Four days later the two younger men returned, and Gareth was still alive. He followed them with his eyes, but it was too much trouble to try and find out what they had done with his package. He must just trust that to God. He had done the best he could. How long it took him to die! Almost as long as it had taken to wait for flying time to come.

When Amory received that package she studied it in astonishment some minutes before she opened it. Who would be sending her a package addressed in an unknown hand?

It looked as if it had been a long journey. It was worn almost through on the corners, and the writing blurred in places as if it had been rained upon, and blistered. It could not belong to her, and yet, there could not be two Amory Lorrimers. That was an unusual name. And Briarcliffe, too! But it bore a New York hotel address at the top of the envelope and the blurred post mark at last gave out the word Alaska!

Then with trembling fingers she tore it open, a wild hope leaping into her heart!

When she brought to light her own little Testament the tears were filling her eyes, glad tears; for whether he were dead or alive it meant that he had thought of her. Or did it? Perhaps he was dead and some one had found the Testament and sent it back to her. But no, he must have addressed it, or at least dictated the address for no one else would know that she was at Briarcliffe unless he told them.

She sat down and turned the pages one by one and saw where they had been read the most; noticed a turned down corner here and there as if to mark a special place, and finally just beyond the words "THE END," she saw a faint impress, like a signature, "Gareth," and a date! How startling! That date was many days after all hope of finding him had been given up. What did it mean?

She compared the writing in the Testament and

the writing on the envelope and was assured they were the same. She sat for a long time with the Testament in her hand thinking it all out, and then she knelt in thanksgiving.

When she rose her eyes were shining.

"I am sure he is alive!" she said aloud.

But it was several hours after that before it became quite clear to her just what she ought to do about it.

She thought first of consulting John Dunleith, but that would mean telling everything to Diana, and she could not do that.

She waited until Mrs. Whitney had gone out to the country club to meet some ladies for tea, and she knew it would be at least two hours before she would return. Neddy and Diana and the minister were down in the woods. They were usually off together somewhere, for Neddy had taken Diana into his heart, and was teaching her how to fish.

She knew that Mr. Whitney was somewhere about the house, and quietly she took the Testament with its wrappings and went to seek him.

She found him on the east porch by himself, surrounded by a sheaf of newspapers, and puffing at one of his big black cigars.

It took a good deal of courage to interrupt him, but when he saw her approaching he looked up pleasantly.

"May I bother you a minute or two with something, Mr. Whitney?" she asked shyly.

"No bother at all, Miss Lorrimer," smiled Whitney genially. "Sit down. There's a chair. Just as easy to sit as stand!"

Amory sat down, her cheeks very pink and her eyes very bright.

"Something has happened," she began, "that I think perhaps some one ought to know, but I shouldn't like everyone to know."

He looked at her keenly.

"I see," he said in a low tone, "You want me to keep it under my hat. I don't blame you in a house like this, whatever it is. You may trust me. What is it? Some of the servants been doing something they ought not to? Some one been bothering you?"

"Oh, no, Mr. Whitney," said Amory trying to get courage to say what she had planned. "It's nothing like that. It's not about me at all. It's about Mr. Kingsley. You see I—knew him—a little!"

Amory had thought this over carefully and decided that this at least was a truthful statement.

But the master of the house frowned a bit anxiously.

"You mean Teddy?" he asked flinging down his paper and watching her. "You *knew* him?"

"Yes," said Amory hurrying on, "and when he went away he took a little Testament of mine with him."

"The dickens he did?" exclaimed Gareth's uncle in surprise, "Ted with a Testament! Well, that's news, anyway! Well, what about it?" He shot her another glance, wondering what this mysterious revelation was anyway.

"Well, you see, to-day it came back!"

"Came back?"

"Yes, came back to me through the mail!"

"You don't say!" said Whitney sitting up very straight. "Where from? Do you know?"

Was this girl trying to put something over on him?

"Why, it was wrapped in a New York hotel envelope, but the post mark is Alaska, somewhere in Alaska. I can't make it all out."

"You don't say!" said Whitney, excitedly. "Have you got that envelope with you? Can I see it? I'd like to see it? I'd like to see the Testament too if you don't mind."

He studied the wrapper carefully and then turned to examine the book. He read Amory's name on the fly leaf, lingered over it in fact, and then slowly turned the pages, noting the marked passages.

"Well, I suppose the explanation is simple enough," he said. "Somebody probably picked this up, some of the fliers who found the plane, maybe, and mailed it to you. It is interesting to have it back of course, but nothing to worry about."

"Yes, but there is a date at the end," explained Amory anxiously, "and the date is only two days before those fliers were there; and I'm almost sure he wrote it himself! He signed his name."

Whitney fluttered the leaves to the end and found the penciled lines.

"Why, what's this?" said the man. "Gareth! That's not his name! He's Theodore!"

"Gareth was the name his mother used to call him," explained Amory gently. "I don't think most people knew him by that name." She had thought this all out and knew it was the only way to explain her part in the matter.

Whitney looked at her with interest.

"Oh, I see! And he asked you to call him by that name? H'm! But say, wasn't that the name they found carved on the plane, some queer sentence; wasn't it Gareth?"

Amory's cheeks were pink but she answered with dignity, "Yes, Mr. Whitney."

"Well, say, why didn't you come forward and explain that when the whole world was in a rumpus about it?"

"Why, I—I didn't see that it would help anything. It couldn't possibly help to find him. They knew it was his plane without that identification. And I thought—it might be misunderstood!"

She was looking him bravely in the eyes and he warmed to her story.

"I see," he said, "and that's why you want me to keep this under my hat too, is it?"

"If you feel that you can, Mr. Whitney."

"I sure can, and I sure will!" he said heartily. "There are too many cats around this house to set one of them on a poor little brave mouse like you. I certainly honor you for your courage and self control. And now, what do you think I ought to do about this? I know you have some idea up your sleeve or you would not have come to me now."

"I don't want you to do anything unless you think you ought to. I just wasn't sure, that's all!"

"But what was your idea?"

"Well, I couldn't help thinking that he might be alive somewhere, and maybe needing some help, and I didn't want to take the responsibility of keeping this to myself. But I do hope nobody else will have to know about it. We were—just good friends— you know."

"I see," said Whitney eyeing her with growing admiration. "Well, I think Ted was very fortunate to have a friend like you. I'll take care, however, that nobody else knows anything about this. You think he's alive, don't you?"

Amory looked up with a lighting of her eyes.

"I can't help but feel that way sometimes."

"Well, I've had a sneaking thought like that myself sometimes. It's like Ted to shut his mouth till he's good and ready to appear again, say he's been hurt or sick or anything Well, we'll see. Do you happen to know whether there are any of the folks around? I'd like a little privacy around that telephone booth if it is a possible thing."

"I think the girls have gone to the country club

with Mrs. Whitney," said Amory, "and Mr. Dunleith and Miss Dorne are with Neddy somewhere."

"Good! Then you stick around near by while I telephone. I might want to ask you a question."

Amory, lingering in the hall, heard the master of the house telephoning to New York.

"Yes, this is Whitney. I'm still thinking of sending out that search expedition, but I want it done in strict privacy, see? No broadcasting or newspapers butting in. And I've got a line on something that makes me think the boy's alive perhaps, but I wouldn't have Mrs. Whitney get onto it for the world till we're sure. She's too nervous to be stirred up again. So keep this strictly under your hat. Yes, something new has happened. I don't mind telling if you keep it to yourself. Don't even let Mallory know. He can't keep his mouth shut. But you see it's this way. A member of the family has received a little book through the mail that Ted had with him, and it's postmarked Alaska, and addressed in his own handwriting. Looks like a new line, doesn't it? But it may be just another false alarm. However, go ahead and get busy. I'll run up to-morrow and tell you more, if I can get away without exciting suspicion. Mrs. Whitney is in a terribly nervous state you know, and it wouldn't do to excite her hopes again. It might prove serious. Yes, he was her favorite nephew."

When Whitney came out of the telephone booth he smiled at Amory.

"There, little girl, I've set that ball rolling, and we'll find that kid if we have to comb the whole of Alaska. I have a hunch that you're right, but keep it under your hat, and I'll do the same. Even if he is 'just a friend' as you say, I guess it hasn't been an easy time for you all these weeks. You've been a brave little girl and I don't mind saying I'm glad you're in our house."

Amory went to her room with shining eyes and a heart more at rest than it had been since Gareth's disappearance. In fact there seemed to be a song bird down in her being somewhere that was singing at the top of his lungs: "Darling! Darling! Darling!" and she pressed her hand over the silver wings hiding over her heart and rejoiced.

CHAPTER XVII

THE next morning at the breakfast table Henry Whitney laid down his newspaper and addressed his wife.

"Where's that secretary of yours, Leila? Can she take dictation? I'd like her to get out a few letters this morning if you don't need her all the time."

Leila Whitney laid down her lorgnette thoughtfully and reflected.

"Well," she said, "I was going to ask her to run into town and do a few errands for me, but if you need her, of course that can wait till afternoon. There really isn't any reason why you shouldn't have her do something for you now and then. I have had so little work for her during this enforced quiet that I'm afraid she'll get lazy. It never does to be too easy on servants."

"I shouldn't call her a servant, if you ask me.

However, that's your business. All I want won't take her half an hour, and then she can go to the city if you like. Send her to me in the library."

So Amory went down and took down three or four letters in short hand, business matters, that did not seem important, and when she was done and about to leave the room Whitney said:

"Oh, by the way. Three of Ted's friends start this afternoon in their own planes for Alaska. They're taking a doctor and medicines and food and all sorts of contrivances to bring him back in case they find him sick or disabled. I thought you'd like to know."

She thanked him with such a shining look that after she was gone he sat reflectively looking off at the sky, and said to himself:

"Friend of hers! H'm! Yes, I guess he is!"

The days passed, and Amory prayed.

Life at the mansion went on much as it had all summer, save that Mrs. Whitney kept talking about moving into town for the winter, and the girls were planning large festivities ahead.

Amory was busier than ever, for now Mr. Whitney had taken to having her work for him an hour or two every morning. He found her swift accuracy, and her clear common sense a great help in getting rid of a lot of begging letters that were constantly pouring down upon him. She seemed to know by instinct just which ones were frauds and which were real worthy cases.

But save for an occasional, "Nothing new yet," when he met her questioning eyes, Whitney had not mentioned the expedition again.

And Amory asked no questions. It was not her place. She had done her duty, and now there was nothing left but to pray. But daily she rejoiced that she had been led to go to Mr. Whitney instead of his wife with her perplexity. In fact, she felt that if it had come to that she would have had to keep the whole matter to herself. Mrs. Whitney would have been simply incapable of seeing anything but wrong in any acquaintance between her secretary and her beloved nephew.

Sometimes as she sat in her lovely room at work, and glanced up toward the mountains in the distance where she had watched Gareth sail away, she wondered what would happen if he should really be alive and come home?

And then she put the thought from her as unworthy. She had nothing whatever to do with that. If Gareth was saved, really saved to all eternity, and if he came home alive, she could be happy no matter what came next. It was a great thing to be glad for, and she would not let it be spoiled. Little details like what Mrs. Whitney might say if the young man acknowledged his friendship with her were too trivial to be counted.

Then she would remind herself that she was in all probability thinking about a man whose body was beneath the icy waters of an Arctic sea; a man the world counted dead and buried and enrolled with bygone heroes. Why would her heart persist in thinking he was alive?

It happened one day when she sat by her window quietly working just as she had dreamed it might do. She glanced up from her desk, and there in the distance came a speck that widened into a great bird, wafting silver wings.

She drew her hand across her eyes to dispel the vision that had been there so many times in imagination that it seemed to be stamped upon her retina.

But the vision was coming on, nearer and nearer, and she could hear the hum of a great motor sailing through the sky.

She put down her pen for her hand was trembling,

and her lips had that weak trembly feeling that comes with sudden excitement.

On came the great bird, as one had come once before on the first night of her arrival, and slowly swung and glided lower. It was going to land! Yes, it was almost down, and she could see some one in it, two persons! Oh, she must not tremble so. In any event she was not down there. She would not have to appear. She would just stay here and get calm. No one would know in the least that she was interested.

The girls were rushing out from the house now. Mrs. Whitney was on the terrace with strained startled face. She could see Diana and John Dunleith hurrying from the woods, with Neddy sprinting ahead. Yes, there was Mr. Whitney coming out on the terrace, a smile of anticipation on his face. Why, could he have expected this arrival? She must get calm. Her heart was beating wildly. At most it was probably only one of Gareth's friends come to report on a fruitless search. She must remember that no one knew of the search but herself and Mr. Whitney.

And now the fliers were coming through the garden gate. She strained her eyes to see, forgetting that she must not be seen, she leaned far out and looked as the two men in fliers' helmets walked up the garden path between the late fall flowers that nodded so gayly in the autumn sunshine.

It was then, just as he passed out from under the big maple tree that he looked up and looked straight into her eyes and smiled. Just as he had done before! Oh, was it his spirit she was seeing? She must not, must not— But ah! The others were looking up also. She drew back quickly, but not before her eyes had given him a shy answering glance.

It was himself, his blessed self, walking in the flesh! Those blue eyes could belong to no other!

She got herself behind the curtain just in time, and saw him greeting the others. She saw that he was thinner with a ghastly pallor, and did not stand quite as jauntily as before, but his grin was the same and his dear blue eyes. He stooped and kissed his aunt and cousins, shook hands with his uncle, slapped the panting Neddy on the shoulder, and then he turned back to his aunt again, with a slight lifting of his eyes to the window above.

"Aunt Leila, you've got my best girl here somewhere. Won't you call her, please? I really can't wait another minute to see her."

Mrs. Whitney's face was a study with various emotions struggling together like scrimmage in a football game.

"Oh, my dear Teddy!" she began in dismay, "I'm afraid you'll be disappointed. She is not—"

"Don't tell me she isn't here!" he cried. "Why, I understood it was a permanent arrangement."

Leila Whitney raised her eyes and saw Diana and John just entering the garden gate.

"Oh yes, Diana is *here*," she answered sweetly, "but, Teddy dear—"

"Oh, is Diana here *too?*"

Gareth wheeled and held out a thin white hand.

"Congratulations, Di, I heard the glad news up in New York on the way down. You couldn't get a better man than my cousin John, and now you're my cousin too, aren't you. For that I shall kiss you!" and he stooped and gave her a resounding smack, and then turning to John with his dear old grin he took his hands in both of his and gave him a grip so fierce that one would never suspect he had been lying at death's door for weeks.

"John, old boy! I'm glad you've got her. She's a highflier but you'll make her what she ought to be. I suspect she needed you all along!"

Amid the somewhat puzzled laughter that followed, the returned wanderer wheeled back to his aunt.

"But I want Amory Lorrimer, Aunt Leila, where are you hiding her? They told me she was still here. You didn't know it, but she's my best girl! We've been friends for quite a while now. If I'd known I was going to make such a long trip of it I'd have told you before I left."

He had done it. He had kept his word and told before them all that she was his friend! That was all he meant of course, just friends. Best girl didn't mean a thing in common parlance to-day; but Amory hiding rosy and startled behind her curtain told herself that she must not let her heart presume upon a word he had said. He was only vindicating her character in case any one had found out about the Testament and the wings.

But Mrs. Whitney was standing there bewildered, utterly undone.

"Why, Teddy! Teddy, dear! You don't mean it! Miss Lorrimer? Why yes, there's a Miss Lorrimer here, I don't remember her first name. She has been my secretary all summer. She is a very nice girl of course, but you have got people mixed. She couldn't really be the one you think."

"Sure she is, Aunt Leila. She's the one all right. Name of Amory. Sweetest name in all the world. Of course I should have told you sooner, only I expected to be right back when I left her. You ought to feel honored to have a secretary like that. Sure, she's my best girl, that is if she hasn't got tired waiting for me while I basked in snow huts and hobnobbed with the eskimos. For sweet mercy's sake, Aunt Leila, won't you call her?"

"Tell Christine to call Miss Lorrimer," said Leila

Whitney to Doris, "quickly!" And just so readily did
Aunt Whitney adjust herself to the occasion.

Wide eyed and shy and frightened Amory came
down. She stepped out upon the terrace before them
all. What was he going to do? How was she going to
act? Would she ever be able to get across the five
feet to where he stood and shake hands formally and
get back again without falling to pieces? Her knees
were wobbling under her, and her eyes would shine
with that unspeakable, indecent joy. They would all
see, and what would they think of her?

But she got only one step, and Gareth did the rest.
Eagerly he came toward her and stooping, touched
his lips with reverence to her forehead, then her lips,
and took her in his arms, half fearfully, as if now
he were here he was not sure she would like it. Suddenly it came to him that praying for a fellow when
he was in danger was one thing, and giving one's
self to him forever might be quite another thing. He
was stricken shy, as he gathered her possessively and
looked down into her eyes.

But there in her eyes he read his answer. It was
unmistakable, and a glad light answered in his own.

He lifted his head with his arm still around her
and said, with a sweeping glance about the astonished company, "Meet my girl, folks! There isn't
another like her in the whole world, and I've seen
a lot of 'em." Then turning to his uncle he said:

"Say, Uncle Henry, can't you arrange for me to
get mother's jewels out of the vault in the city? I
want to get my trademark on this hand so there
won't be any more mistakes made! And now, for
sweet mercy's sake, let me sit down. I haven't stood
up so long since I left the old bird on the ice berg,
and I'm just about all in. Got a glass of milk, Aunt
Leila, I'm still on baby food!"

With the old grin still on his thin white face, the old light in his eyes, his arm still tight around his "best girl," he walked unsteadily into the house and dropped down on the couch, pulling Amory down beside him.

They all began to rush here and there to get pillows to put behind him, to bring him a glass of milk, and a cup of coffee, and a stool for his feet, and to take his helmet from him; Amory, with blazing cheeks, and happy eyes, tried to get up and do something for him too, but he held her fast.

"No, you're not going, little girl," he said. "Get out of here, all of you people, can't you, and let us have a few minutes to ourselves? Where's my pilot? Did you leave him outside? Go out and give him a little of this attention. He's worked hard to bring me here and he deserves it."

Uncle Henry Whitney stood in the door with a "this-my-son" smile on his face, and now he stepped in and shooed them all out.

"Now," said Gareth, eagerly drawing Amory close when they were at last alone, "did you get my message? The one I scratched on the plane? They told me up in New York that it was broadcasted over the earth. Did you get it, Amory? And did you understand?"

He looked hungrily into her eyes, and did not miss their answer.

"Darling!" he said softly, putting his face down to hers, "darling! You didn't mind me calling you that over the phone, did you?—Darling!"

"Oh, no!" said Amory burying her happy face in his shoulder. "Oh, no! I—*loved* it!"

Then her hands stole up and around his neck, and she whispered softly in his ear:

"Gareth! *Child of God!*"